the gates of ivory,
the gates of horn

the gates of ivory,
the gates of horn

Thomas McGrath

**PUBLISHED BY
ANOTHER CHICAGO PRESS
CHICAGO**

Published in the United States by
Another Chicago Press, PO Box 11223, Chicago, IL 60611.

Cover design by Josie Taglienti

This project is funded in part by
a grant from the Illinois Arts Council.

Library of Congress Catalog Card Number: 87-72336

ISBN: 0-9614644-2-9

Distributed by
Illinois Literary Publishers Association
Post Office Box 816
Oak Park, Illinois 60303

For Alice—discoverer of the Unoccupied Country

INTRODUCTION

Thomas McGrath is above all else a poet. He is the author of a number of major works of poetry, in particular
the long poem, *Letter To An Imaginary Friend* (Parts
One and Two, Swallow Press, 1970, 1972; Parts
Three and Four, Copper Canyon, 1985). It is surely as
a poet that his reputation has been made, and it is as a
poet that he will be given his greatest recognition. In my
view, McGrath's reputation is only now beginning to
spread to the larger poetry-reading public, many years
after he made his appearance as the first of the poets
published by Alan Swallow in that significant poetry
publishing enterprise. Although he has been the recipi-
ent of a number of important poetry prizes, such wider
recognition has escaped him, in part, I believe, because
of a kind of residual McCarthyism— for McGrath has
consistently and steadfastly maintained with pride his
connection with the political left. Testifying as an
unfriendly witness before the late and unlamented
House Committee on Un-American Activities in 1952,
while he was on the faculty of Los Angeles State University, McGrath replied to a question about his political connections that he belonged to the "unaffiliated far
left." That and other such comments cost him his faculty job, and led to a number of years of work at many
pursuits not terribly conducive to the writing of poetry.
He worked in a factory that made toy animals, wrote
some film scripts—tried to keep body and soul together,

while continuing his work on his long poem and on other poetry as well.

The novel here was written during this period of McGrath's life, or just after it, and has upon it the hallmarks of the McCarthy era. Its close cousins are such other dystopias as *Brave New World* and *1984,* but unlike especially the first of these works, it is written by one who *personally faced* the investigators, and wouldn't knuckle under to them. That the novel makes its reappearance during the height of the Reagan era, when the United States Government is again seeing reds under every bed—or Sandinistas at our doorstep, or terrible threats form a novelist like Margaret Randall, to whom citizenship is denied and who is threatened with deportation—is a credit to the editors of Another Chicago Press.

The function of this introduction is two-fold—to tell potential readers of the novel a little about its author, and to place the novel in the time frame in which it made its first appearance. First, then, a little more about the poet and here the novelist, Thomas McGrath:

McGrath was born in 1916 in Sheldon, North Dakota, into a sizable farm family. He went to school in Sheldon and surroundings, worked on the farm, learned the lore of the Native Americans who had been displaced from that part of the nation, and eventually, after some false starts and with little money, he went to college, first at Morehead State University just across the state line into Minnesota, and later at the University of North Dakota. That he was a good student is adequately demonstrated by the fact that in his final year he won a Rhodes Scholarship. Because World War II had broken out, it was impossible for the Rhodes Scholars to go to England to study at Oxford, but they received invitations to study from many Universities in the United States, and McGrath accepted one from Louisiana State University, in part because Baton Rough was so different from North Dakota. He studied especially under Cleanth Brooks, who took the Rhodes Scholars on campus under his wing. He also met Alan Swallow, who was already engaged in the publishing enterprise which was to play such a significant role in American poetry publishing. He and McGrath became friends, and Swallow published McGrath's first book, and published his work as well in collections with other poets. McGrath was already a political activist.

At the end of his time in Baton Rouge McGrath took a teaching job at a small college in Maine. Not happy with his situation, he moved to New York, where he worked in a shipyard and was involved in organizing. Eventually, he joined the Army. Most of his time in the service was spent in the Aleutian Islands, where, he says, the threat of dying from boredom was greater than the threat of dying from gunfire. It was only after the end of the war that McGrath was able to take advantage of his Rhodes Scholarship, spending two years at Oxford, and traveling extensively on the Continent. Returning to the United States, he took the job at Los Angeles State already mentioned, faced down the Un-Americans, and scuffled for a living as did so many others during that particularly ugly moment in American history.

In time, McGrath was to resume his teaching career, ending it at his retirement from Morehead State University in 1983. The list of his publications during these years is extensive. In addition to the long and central poem of his *ouvre* cited earlier, there are many other books of poetry, early on one of my own favorite titles, *Longshot O'Leary's Garland of Practical Poesie* (International Publishers, 1949), more recently, *Passages Toward the Dark* (Copper Canyon Press, 1982), or *Echoes Inside the Labyrinth* (Thunder's Mouth Press, 1983). The publication in 1985 of Parts Three and Four of *Letter To An Imaginary Friend* was a signal event indeed in a most important career. At least one volume of commentary and other material related to McGrath has been published, an issue of *North Dakota Quarterly* guest-edited by Fred Whitehead and entitled *The Dream Champ*. McGrath has been associated with a number of journals and "little"magazines, most important perhaps the journal *Crazy Horse* edited by him and his then-wife, Eugenia. He has also served on the editorial board of *California Quarterly,* and on the Board of the journal *Mainstream,* which was later for a short while to combine under the title *Masses and Mainstream,* with the *New Masses,* that important, frankly "left" publication which fell on economically hard days during the McCarthy era.

McGrath is the father of a son, Tomasito, who plays a significant, muse-like role in some of the later poetry. After his retirement from Morehead State, McGrath took up residence in Minneapolis—perhaps because his brother Martin lives there—and continues to write. It is only now that recognition, and some well-deserved kudos are coming his way.

The novel before us was first published in 1957, by

Mainstream Publishers, the publishing house associated with the journal *Mainstream*. One must imagine the political situation in the United States at the time of its publication to understand the force of the novel, and the fact that it had to be published by a small left-wing publishing house is part of that situation. Nothing of which most readers are likely to be aware will make clearer how the world must have seemed to a young left-wing poet in the 'fifties, than that Julius and Ethel Rosenberg had not only been convicted, but had been executed as spies by the government, in a trial so flawed that controversy about it continues to this day. The House Committee on Un-American Activities went from town to town with its circus, calling witnesses for no other purposes than to get headlines, and to send some people to jail—always for the crime of "contempt of Congress," never for any criminal or even political actions. Senator Joseph McCarthy was riding high with his denunciations based on little or nothing, and even so respectable a figure as Attorney General Herbert Brownell, Jr., in 1953 leveled charges against former President Harry Truman to the effect that Truman had promoted Harry Dexter White—who, Brownell insisted, with no evidence, was a Russian spy—to the International Monetary Fund. It is obviously not appropriate here to write a history of the 'fifties, but it seems to me important to realize that the atmosphere in the United States, in the aftermath of World War II, in the aftermath of Russian development of atomic weapons, in the aftermath perhaps especially of the war in Korea—was one which might make the inquisitorial state presented in McGrath's novel seem like a real possibility. The left was thoroughly isolated and discredited in this situation, and the Communist left in particular was isolated. Little wonder that a poet like McGrath could find no publishers outside the left to accept his work. Little wonder that the poet's imagination was centered on the effect of mindcontrol and thoughtcontrol on a nation which seemed paranoid.

It does not seem to me an appropriate function of an introduction to evaluate the work the reader is about to examine. It will have to be each reader's own decision if McGrath's novel is to be read primarily as a document of its own moment, reflecting the particular strains and stresses, the particular injustices and tribulations of the United States of the 'fifties, or if the novel has application in a larger historical framework. Few readers will deny, I think, the notion that the tension between Constitutional guarantees of freedom, and their violation by those in power, are a constant of the American historical experience, especially in a war-like situation like the one the novel portrays. One need only listen to the President of the United States who, as I write this, has just finished telling us that if we do not support the "Contras" who wish to topple the Sandinista regime in Nicaragua, we face the loss of the continent to the "Russian conspiracy."

Each reader of this novel will also have to evaluate the importance of the work as a work of fiction. That it stands in the now well-established tradition of the dystopic novel, that is, the novel which gives us precisely the opposite of a utopian world, is a place to begin. That such novels are very much a part of the literature of our century is undoubtedly true, as the near-classics in English I have already mentioned establish. Such works continue to appear, in underground publications or in more public and open ways, all demonstrating that the issues McGrath's novel raises continue to be issues of major concern in much of present day world, nearly 30 years after *The Gates of Ivory, The Gates of Horn* made its first appearance. For all such works, one's judgement of their value will depend in part on one's judgement of the political situation, in part on one's sense of the function of fiction. For myself, the importance of the novel lies in its ability to give us another insight into the ideas, the language, the development of a writer I think of as one of the most important of contemporary American poets.

Frederick C. Stern

University of Illinois at Chicago

Two gates the silent house of sleep adorn:
Of polished ivory this, that of transparent horn;
True visions through transparent horn arise;
Through polished ivory pass deluding lies.

THE AENEID, Book **VI.**
Dryden's translation

THE GATES OF IVORY, THE GATES OF HORN

By Thomas McGrath

I.

"Not guilty."

The Umpire put his hand under the edge of his desk and a great peony of light swam up out of the space above his head, sharpened into focus and drilled at the suspect.

"Again?"

"Not guilty!"

"Your pigeon," the Umpire said and turned his heavy head, his uninterested, blue wide-apart eyes toward the Investigator who sat in what was now almost shadow, a grey man in a grey suit who wore his youngish anonymous face like a mask. "Do you want to play him?"

"Have his Psychomutual score sheets been explained to him?"

"He's seen them." The Umpire turned his head to the Suspect. "Your last chance," he said. "You saw your PM score and you know what it means. Now, do you want to confess and ask for punishment, or do you want to play?"

"Not guilty."

"No choice then," the Investigator said. "Strap him in and call the Witness."

The Umpire left his desk and went over to the Suspect. He touched a button and the metal bands came out, clamping the man's arms and legs. Another button, and a web of wires came down over the Suspect's head and the back of his neck. Like a huge fly in a tiny net the man shook and jerked in the chair; he began to curse in a shaky voice.

"Listen to that, would you?" the Umpire said, indignantly. He went back to his desk and riffled the PM score sheet. "Predictable I suppose. Section 7-34-C— you notice it? Violence."

"Of course," the Investigator said boredly. "It's in all of them. Standard reaction. Probably in your PM sheet too." He paused for a moment to let the Umpire get the full effect of it; then he said coldly: "It's not your job to get involved in this. You're a legal neutral. That's why you're the Umpire, remember?"

"Oh sure," the Umpire gave a little laugh, like the tentative beginning of a scale, but he did not complete it. He glanced at the grey figure of the Investigator in the shadow, as if unsure how to take him. "You're a great kidder," he said, more heavily than he had intended.

"I never joke. The law is a serious thing and it would be a good idea if you were to remember that. Now get the Witness in here."

The Witness was already in the room. His mask gleaming faintly, he came forward to the box at the edge of the little pond of fierce light in which the Suspect floated like a witch on a ducking stool.

18

"Ready," he said.

"You know the Suspect?" the Investigator asked him.

"Yes sir. William Horne. H-O-R-N or H-O-R-N-E. Forty-four Court Street, New Pasadena."

"Smith!" the Suspect said. "My name is William Smith. I just got in from Frisco."

"Court Street is skidrow, isn't it?" the Investigator asked.

"Skidrow, yes sir." The Witness paused a moment. "Forty-four Court is a transient hotel. Mostly for the workless. It's——"

"I'll ask the questions. Speak when you're asked to speak!"

"Yes sir," the Witness said a little breathlessly.

"What is the nature of your charge against Mr. Horne?"

"Conspiring, sir."

"General or specific?"

"General, I guess, sir. Yes sir, general."

There was a moment of silence while the Witness squirmed in his chair.

"Sir," he said, "what I mean is——"

The voice of the Investigator lashed at him. "What is your name, Witness?"

"Jones, sir. Ernest M."

"How long have you been working as an Informer?"

"Six—six months, sir. I'm—I'm a Tech Three, sir. I——"

"Don't you know that a charge of general conspiracy does not require the presence of an Informer at the investigation, that a suspect charged with general conspir-

19

acy can be sentenced by an Umpire without hearing, sentence not to exceed twenty-nine years in the Venus Penal Colony, the tapioca swamps?"

"Sir, I——?"

"Better be careful."

It was the Suspect speaking now. "Better be careful, stoolpigeon. You'll be sitting where I'm sitting." He began to laugh.

"Shut up, you!" the Umpire roared at him. "Shut up or I'll juice you!"

"Well, Mister Jones?" the Investigator prodded him.

"It's general, sir—the charge, I mean. But it's also specific."

"Go on."

"Criticizing spellcasts, sir."

"Which ones?"

"All of them. The advertising. He——"

"Criticism of advertising plugs is not a crime. I know there have been cases where it has been punished, by overzealous Investigators. But Philistinism—as the Punishment Department which pays you should have made clear—is characterized as a tendency, not a crime."

"Yes sir, I know that, sir," the Witness said all-in-a-rush. "But he turned one off. Sabotage, sir."

Again there was a moment of silence, through which they could hear the quick, heavy breathing of the Suspect.

"That is serious," the Investigator said, keeping his voice neutral.

"Listen!" the Suspect said. "He's not telling it right! He's——"

"You'll have a chance to reply," the Investigator said, but the Suspect was shouting now and the Investigator could not be sure that he heard.

"Shut up!" the Umpire bellowed again.

"God damn you, don't tell me to shut up! I's *my* life that's at stake! Make him tell the truth, damn him! I——"

The Investigator nodded and the Umpire's hand went forward. There was a momentary crackle, the faintest smell of ozone. A tentacle at the prisoner's neck twitched delicately and the man leaped against the metal clamps and then was still, his breathing harsh and ragged.

"Anything else?" the Investigator asked.

"Yes, sir," the Witness said. "A book."

"Book?"

"History book, sir."

"Well." Again the moment of silence.

"Suspect can read, sir."

"I should suppose so, if he has a book."

"All done?" the Umpire was bored, now that all the evidence was in. He took out a small knife and began cleaning his nails.

"Let him talk."

The Umpire pushed the rheostat control on his desk and the prisoner straightened and his voice bloomed out in a great bush of profanity.

"All right," the Investigator said. "You've heard the evidence against you. What have you to say about it?"

"He's a liar, a damned liar!"

"You saw him turn off the spellcast?" the Investigator asked the Witness.

21

"I'll swear to it."

"Same thing. You have the book, I suppose?"

"Yes sir." The Witness held it up: dark, heavy, uninteresting looking. The print would be too small, the Investigator knew; there would be handwritten notes crammed in the margins, the bottom of every page would be a jungle of footnotes: a dangerous book. Suddenly, inexplicably, he was tired and discouraged.

"Damn you!" the Suspect cursed at the Witness. "Who are you? Take off that mask! I got a right to know who's condemning me!"

"Bastard!" The Umpire dropped his pen-knife and straightened in his seat. His hand flashed to the rheostat. Again the tentacle whipped at the neck of the Suspect and the man leaped in the chair.

"Stop it!" The Investigator stood up at his desk. "You're neutral," he said to the Umpire. "Turn it off. Be neutral."

"You heard him!"

"Yes." He turned to the Suspect. "You know better than to say a thing like that," he said. "You're not allowed to impugn the character of an Informer. That in itself is conspiracy. General conspiracy, it is true, but it doesn't help your case. The profession of Informer is an honorable one and not to be vilified. And the Thirty-Ninth Amendment fully guarantees their rights, one of which is to be masked and anonymous in any investigation. That is why they are all called Jones. Now let's have no more of these outbursts. Do you want to make a statement?"

"Yes." All the fight seemed to have gone from the

Suspect. "I did turn off the spellcast, all right. It was in this hotel on Court Street. I'd just come in from the mountains—trying to kill some deer to take me through the winter. I'm a workless stiff all right and I do field work with the fruit tramps when there's work, but it's hard getting through the winter. So I didn't get anything and I figured to go farther south and try for a job—there's a few places down there where work isn't outlawed—and I was staying at this hotel."

"Briefly, please."

"There was this old bindle stiff there and he was sick and he couldn't sleep with the spellcast on. All of us in the flopjoint felt sorry for him. So I turned it off."

They waited without speaking.

"*Somebody* had to," the Suspect said defiantly.

"And the book?"

"I didn't have any book. It's true I can read, but I didn't have any book. If I did, I'd have sold it in the Black Market. Probably get three, four hundred for a book that thick. I could use the money."

"You deny ownership then?"

"He must have planted it in my stuff."

"Let me have the book."

The Witness handed it across and the Investigator took it, feeling, as he always did when handling a book, a queer tingling in his fingertips; feeling too the momentary surprise he always felt at the materiality of the book, its gross and actual body, as if it should somehow have been formed all of an airy and electric nothing.

He opened the book, holding it so that he could look at the endpapers against the fierce light that shone on the

23

Suspect. Yes, it was there, the stamped P.D., the label of the Punishment Department. It had been efficiently erased, but against the light he could read it clearly. So the Suspect was right, the book had been planted. Damn them, he thought wearily, why can't they once, just once, get a new book and do a decent job? and turning to the Suspect said smoothly:

"There's something here that must have been your signature. It's been erased." And hurried on then so that the Suspect would not begin to shout his denials: "I find that the charge has been sustained. Reason for turning off the spellcast is insufficient. Coupling that with your failure to deny opposition to the advertisements, I can only conclude that you are an information saboteur. Ownership of the book I take as a separate charge. As you know it is not unlawful to own *all* books, although in these days of advanced scientific art, it is certainly bad taste. Ownership of a history book, is, of course, felonious. I have no choice but to condemn you. Have you anything to say?"

"It's a lie! All of you know it's a lie, but still you're going to finish me! Isn't that right?"

"You've been investigated in complete accord with the procedures of the Punishment Department. There is evidence—some of which you have admitted yourself. Even without such evidence, many Investigators would demand your punishment. Considering your attitude and your PM score, apart from all evidence, it is clear in what direction you are tending."

Talking to the Suspect, he forgot the Witness, the planted book, and was, for the first time, really interested

24

in the case. It was clear enough that Horn or Horne or Smith or whatever his name was (Horn was probably a case in the files of the PD which they wanted to close and they were using the Suspect to kill two birds with one stone, he thought) was guilty—if not now, then in a year; if not in act, then in thought; and he wanted the Suspect to understand this. He went on talking to him while the Umpire cleaned his nails and the Witness leaned forward, his mask gleaming, hanging on every word: one day he, too, might be an Investigator.

"You have to understand," the Investigator said, "that in a highly organized society such as ours, one involving hundreds of millions of people and the greatest degree of division of leisure and specialization, it is not possible to allow a wide tolerance for the idiosyncracies of individuals. In a less specialized society, yes; among your friends, hunting in the mountains, yes; but not in ours. You think that we are being vindictive, but we are only trying to save people like yourself from the hazards of their own individuality. If you were my own brother, I would want the same thing for you—for the good of all of us. I am not a vindictive man; I love our country. We must remember the words: *One nation indivisible with efficiency and punishment for all.*"

There was a long pause when he finished. The Umpire put away his pen-knife and yawned delicately.

"You're crazy," the Suspect said finally. "You— why, by God! you want me to *forgive* you—you want me to tell you you're right. Well, you're a monster. You're *not* right. You—oh, Christ, get it over with."

The Umpire looked at the Investigator, shrugging,

and the Witness hunched forward in his chair. The Investigator put his hand under the side of his desk. For just an instant he hesitated, trying to think what he might say that would make it clear, that would explain it all fairly and clearly to the Suspect so that the Suspect might admit that he understood—as the Investigator felt that he himself would understand if he were in the chair and their roles reversed. In that instant he felt an empathy with the Suspect, imagined himself in the chair, and shuddered. His finger went down on the switch.

For a fraction of a second it seemed that nothing would happen. They were all frozen in place like pieces of statuary while the Suspect lolled in his chair. Then he leaped against the metal restrainers, the air hummed briefly, and he was still. The Witness went quickly out, making strangled sounds under his mask, and the Umpire stepped over to the Suspect, folded back an eyelid and nodded.

"Done."

He looked at the Investigator for a long moment, enigmatically, and then shrugged as if shifting something from his back. The Investigator was busying himself filling up his brief case.

"Open and shut," the Umpire said. He shook his heavy head as if to clear it and his eyes became blank and indifferent again.

"What is the name of the Witness?" the Investigator asked.

"Witness? Real name? Oh. Johnson. Martin Johnson. Why?"

"I thought he was pretty bad. I'm wondering about him."

"Yes?" For a moment the Umpire was interested, then he laughed. "New," he said. "Raw. No experience."

"I wondered."

The Umpire laughed again. "Going to investigate him?"

"I might. We have to be sure. We have to suspect everyone."

"Yes."

He watched the grey figure of the Investigator as the man walked across to the door. For just a moment it seemed that the Umpire was on the point of speaking. Then the Investigator was gone. The Umpire began to hum tunelessly through his teeth. He took out his pen-knife again. He held his elbows against his body to keep his hands from shaking.

————o————

The office was at the end of the hall, an unpretentious plate of one-way glass with, painted on it, a picture of a man carrying a huge load of nondescript objects and beside it a realistic, disturbing drawing of an eye, like something out of an oculist's magazine. Printed below the symbols was his name, *John Cary,* and his profession: *Investigator.* He put his thumb against the identifier key and the door swung silently open and he went across to his desk.

It satisfied him. Blank as the moon or the sandy wastes of the Sahara, it seemed all innocence and functional surface, but he was not sure until he had gone over it with a magnifier and an infra-red Tracker. Yes, it was just as he had left it. He put the brief-case on it now and sat down and fumbled in a drawer for his pipe. Lighting it, he saw the flowers.

The match burnt his fingers and the shock of pain pushed back his fear and he got up from the desk and went over to them. Sitting on top of the shimmer of the old-fashioned space-warp filing case, they seemed to hang in the air, remote and impalpable as a dream symbol.

He cut off the field of the case and now, perched on the battered steel boxes of the file, the flowers regained a certain reality. Too much, perhaps. Closer, their perfume was terribly strong, cloying and drug-like, and for a moment he nearly gagged. Then, suddenly, he realized that, barbaric as it was, he liked it, and now he felt an irrational guilt along with his fear. They were roses, he thought, and some lines from a forbidden book floated into his head, borne on the scent of the flowers: *My love is like a red, red rose.* And the commentary on it: "the language is non-symbolic, for no conventional acceptation will make the paraphrase, 'my fiancee is a flower of the genus rosacea var. red' a statement containing the poetic emotion expressed in the original statement"—all meaningless words.

The initial guilt was gone now and he put his mind to the problem of the flowers. Somebody had got into the office, that was plain, and the roses—they were presumably some kind of warning. For a moment the extent of conspiracy and sedition seemed monstrous—too

28

great and pervasive to cope with, but he forced himself to go on thinking.

The flowers would have been terribly expensive—his full week's salary, he thought, wondering how he knew, since he never bought any. Flowers were an enormous luxury now, and buying them constituted a kind of criticism of a society too busy and mechanized to allow them more than marginal existence. Expensive, then. And where would one buy them? There were few shops. One, he remembered, in the financial district of New Wall Street. Another in the suburb where he himself lived. Wild flowers, those were, brought in by trappers and Indians from the Unoccupied Country. . . .

—Why did he feel guilty?

Suddenly he began to laugh. He nuzzled his face into the flowers and took a long dizzying breath and laughed again. Behind him the intercom crackled and popped and Gannell said "I'm coming in." He switched on the field, the files disappeared in their watery shimmer, and he picked the vase of flowers from their top and carried them over to his desk. He was still chuckling, lighting his pipe, when his assistant came into the room.

At forty, Gannell, head of the technical section and second in command to Cary, was hardly older than his Chief, but he looked older. He looked like a piece of eroded sculpture, Cary thought; the bald, beaked, owlish head of a totem-pole.

"Hello, Gannell," Cary said.

"Hello, John. And congratulations on that thing this afternoon. Nicely handled."

"Thanks. It's tiresome work."

"Tiresome?"

"I mean all the work that goes into it. All the energy of Umpires and Stoolpigeons and Investigators—the Punisment Department organization, the Legal Corps—all that. And all simply to juice a workless unimportant man. It doesn't seem very efficient, sometimes."

"I see what you mean. Still, it has to be done."

"Yes. But at the cost of all that effort? Take this one this afternoon. Probably not even guilty as charged. Of course by extrapolation we know that he *was* guilty, either now or next week, but look at the work to convict!"

"Form," Gannell said. "Got to be done with proper form. By the way, what's this the Umpire said about your questioning the Witness?"

"Something about him seemed wrong." Cary fiddled with his pipe, thinking of how might be the best way to put it. "Look," he said. "I know that the best kind of Informer is the paranoid, and I know that the profession of Informer has made it possible to create a real economic function for this kind of psycho. But there was something haywire about this one. Too clumsy. You know how a schizo is—all cleverness and assurance. Not this one. So I wondered."

"Yes?" Gannell looked at him curiously.

"I was thinking—do you suppose that a sane one might have slipped through on us?"

"Not likely. Do you suspect him?"

"We have to suspect everyone. Even ourselves."

"Oh, but——" Gannell's rock-like head came up. Like a long-necked dinosaur he had been feeding on the bottom-grass of his own problems while the waters of the conversation lapped above his head. "What do you mean by that, John?"

"Just thinking. This case this afternoon had to do with a fellow who turned off a spellcast. Supposed to have had a history book too, but that was planted, I think. Well, everybody has a certain happiness-quota and watching spellcasts is an acceptable way of filling it. But have you noticed how *much* people watch them? Riding home at night on the freeway, that's all they do."

"But that's what they *should* do!"

"Sure. But how many hours can you spend at spellcasts without it's becoming an inverted criticism of the culture? When does it become an *avoidance* of responsibility?"

"I see what you mean," Gannell said thoughtfully. The heavy face, like a stone bird, brooded on the egg of the problem.

"Even ourselves are suspect," Cary said. "Notice these?" He gestured at the flowers.

"Oh. Wondered what that bad smell was. Roses, aren't they? How did they get here?"

"Me. *I* bought them. Brought them in and forgot about them—had a pretty bad time for a while—thought somebody had been in the office—couldn't recall for several minutes that I'd bought them myself."

Gannell again looked at him as if Cary had been just newly born in the chair in front of him.

"Well," he said. "At last! I thought you were made out of steel, but you're human after all."

"What?"

"You've finally done it—overworked yourself. Happens to all of us after a while in this business. So much suspicion, I suppose. We get so that even our own acts seem questionable. Then we begin to forget them. Occupational fatigue. *Virus Investigatoris*, I call it—and I hope you won't begin to look at me suspiciously because I know a bit of another language. Well, John, after all these years you're finally going to have to take a vacation."

"I suppose so. But, damn it, the flowers——"

"Don't worry about them. After all, they're not seditious."

"They're questionable."

"Not in relation to *you*," Gannell said, laughing.

"I laughed too. But it's not funny. I don't like that side of myself."

"Fatigue."

"Yes. But it shows something weak."

"For God's sake man, if we begin to doubt ourselves, where are we at? A moment ago you talked of all the work that goes into a juicing. Inference: we should be allowed to juice when we think necessary—be Witness and Umpire and Punisher all rolled into one. But how in the name of heaven can we do that if we doubt our *own* motives? The next step would be a failure to convict *anyone*, since if our own motives are suspect there is absolutely *nothing* in the world to sanction our judgments and our actions."

"Perhaps if there were something outside us—if the law were really absolute—even more absolute than the Political Corporation——"

"Now there you *are* on dangerous ground," Gannell said quietly. "*Whose* absolute would it be?"

"Yes," Cary said. He thought of the Suspect and the millions like him and felt again, as he had when he had first seen the flowers, the sense of heaviness, almost of defeat, imagining a plot as pervasive and impalpable as fog. "Yes, I suppose you're right."

"Hell, yes, I'm right," Gannell said, and his face unlocked itself in a grin like a mortal wound. "You're beat out and you need a rest. But first I've got something for you. It's absolutely got to get done, orders from on high, but you should make it your last piece of business. Finish it and order yourself to rest for a while."

"What is it?"

Gannell zipped open a briefcase and tossed a file on the desk.

"Look."

The fact that looked out at him from the file of papers was like a spirit photograph, amorphous as a face in a dream; but it hit him like a fist in the guts. He felt his heart like a great bird in the cage of his ribs and his throat tightened as if he were being garroted.

"It's—it's——"

"Yeah. Your twin brother. Bad picture, but the infra-red went haywire somehow. One of these trap-cameras and they never work well."

Cary managed to get control of his voice.

"What did he do?"

"Anti-culturalist. Smuggles books into libraries."

"But——"

"That's only the beginning. He's suspected of blowing

33

up spellcast stations, organizing emigration to the Unoccupied Territory—somewhere in the Dakotas, I think—all sorts of things. But most important, he's suspected of being the leader of the seditionist movement here in L.A. Chief conspirator. How long since you've seen him?"

"Years," Cary said mechanically. "I thought he was dead."

"I *wish* he were. You have any objections to working on the case?"

"No." He considered it for a moment and all he felt was a dull anger—against the investigation of the afternoon, the intolerance of the Suspect who had refused to see his argument, the Witness, the flowers: against himself. If there could only be an end to it, he thought; if we could only get them all. "No. No objection."

"Good. I was sure there wouldn't be. After all, one may have several brothers, but accurate punishment—that's another thing. I can tell you that this is pretty big, John. Get him and you'll put an end to their activity in L.A."

"*If* there's an end." He saw the question in Gannell's face. "A line has an end," he said. "But a circle doesn't. A river has, but not the ocean."

"I see what you mean." Gannell was no longer listening; once more he browsed on the bottom grass. "Get this one and you'll end it," he said. "Be careful of the material in that dossier. It took the PD three years and about fifty million dollars to get it."

"I'll put in in the time-file," Cary said. He glanced briefly through the folder, feeling a dull anger, first at

34

Chris, the blacksheep twin, and then, irrationally, at Gannell; feeling something else as well, something he couldn't place—fear? guilt?

The odor of the roses was oppressive. He shoved them across the desk and picked up the folder and carried it across the room.

The time-file was at the other end. It looked like an old-fashioned post-office box except for the doubling of verniered dials on its small door. He put his hand out——

All space seemed to fold roaring around him, the marrow in his bones froze, and, in the absolute black of space, suns flared and died like a shower of sparks as he thought desperately *O God I'm lost,* and irrelevantly (from some forbidden book) *shattered glass and toppling masonry, and time one livid final flame* and for an endless instant he was certain that he was dead and he felt, then, as he had when, a boy, his father had punished him: content.

Then he felt himself shouting *no!* but there was no voice.

White faced, Gannell stared at him from near the desk, trying to speak. He made a strangling sound:

"It's—it's——"

Cary felt coherence coming back into himself. He backed away from the machine, feeling himself begin to shake all through as if he were compounded of jelly.

"Booby-trapped," he said. "Somebody set it for maximum and I triggered it off when I moved the dial." He put his back against the wall and tried to make the trembling stop. "How'd I get back?"

35

Gannell took a long breath. "They didn't do a good job of it, I suppose. Or you didn't move the dial far enough or something. Christ!—the whole end of the room seemed gone—nothing but darkness." He shuddered.

Cary was looking at the mechanism. "You're right," he said. "It's been tinkered with. But who?" He did not spend any time thinking about it—there were enough people who might want to send him out into that darkness. "The dossier," he said. "The data you gave me." He had a momentary vision of the papers in that dossier falling like snow through the roof of some unknown room. In the past? The future? The shaking began all over again.

"Don't worry about the dossier," Gannell told him. The heavy man was business-like again. "We're damn lucky we can replace it. Sorry about this, John—never saw this kind of ambush before. Kind of compliment to you, in a way."

"I can do without them."

"So can I," Gannell said, laughing. "Now, why don't you knock off for the day? I'll send a précis of the material in the dossier over to your place."

"All right."

"Crack this one in a hurry and go on that long vacation."

"Sure."

Cary had a feeling of such tiredness that he felt he could never again be rested. He picked up his briefcase, shuffled some papers into it, and reached for his hat.

"You want these?" Gannell gestured at the roses.

"No." The fragrance of the flowers now seemed sickening to Cary.

"I'll get rid of them."

Gannell took the flowers out of the vase and carried them to the time-file. He opened the door, tossed the flowers inside, flipped the door shut and spun the dials.

"Always get a kick out of this," he told Cary. "Got one of these time-file gadgets at home. They really work perfectly as a garbage disposal unit. If we can ever get the price down on them, everybody'll have one. And sometime they'll build them big enough for time travel."

"I suppose so. Where did you send them?"

"Oh, the future, of course. Can't tell what sort of change it might make if we sent them into the past. Always send stuff to the distant future."

"But what about its effect there?"

"Oh, well," Gannell laughed, "we can't be worried about that, can we? It's *now* that's important." Still laughing he followed Cary out of the room.

———o———

Now it was night and there was a strong wing blowing. Now he came out of the building and onto the open belt-line and pulled on his goggles to protect his eyes against the smog. Now it was at·least breathable, so that he did not need the gas-mask, and, on impulse, he decided to walk to the car-creche. The beltline was covered with a scatter of homeward-going workers, most of them from the great buildings that pushed into the murky sky along all the streets. He joined them now, a youngish man of middle height with brown nondescript hair and a face that was neither handsome nor homely, carrying his fear with him like a man with a live grenade in his pocket. Riding the beltline, leaping from slow to fast channels and back again, working himself toward his destination, did not give him time to think. At the end of the line he took the narrow seldom-used sidewalk to the corner, turned it and paused automatically to see if he were being followed.

It was getting dark now. Like tired fireflies the windows of the huge buildings winked and went out, and only the phallic monolith of Amalgamated Joy was still lighted. It seemed to Cary that it was on fire, burning, that it would consume the city. He pushed the notion away with a tired vehemence, recording automatically against himself that it was a seditious thought, and then attempted to discount it, as he had the flowers, on the ground that he was worn out, needed a rest.

But the tiredness, the forgetting—that, too, was suspect. An image, blown in perhaps on the wind from the desert, the wind which had cleared out a part of the smog, grew in his mind: snakes in a pit, biting each other, the last snake biting at his own tail, swallowing itself——

He shuddered and pushed the thought out of his head, thinking of the town on its narrow shelf between the sea and the desert, between the fixed death of the bleached skulls and wind-warped stone of the desert, and the chaotic turbulence and swarming life of the sea. He hated the wind.

Sticks tapped on the street. Suddenly he was clear-headed and competent again and he put his back against

38

the building, his hand on the B-gun, and waited.

Dry and insect-like, the sound approached. The man came around the corner, his white cane clapping the sidewalk briskly. Clipped to his head, directly in front of his eyes, the tiny spellcast screen blazed with white light. It was one of the Hands.

"Halt!"

"Yes, sir?"

The Hand paused and his stick went out like a stiffened tentacle, but he did not turn off the spellcast. He's disciplined, Cary thought approvingly; but he kept his voice cold.

"What are you doing out at this time of the night?"

"Going home, sir. I've got a work permit, sir. Half hour a day——"

"You're not allowed out after dark."

"Permission, sir. Gave me permission to walk home. I had my spellcast going, sir."

"Right." Cary took the paper the man passed across, glanced at it, and handed it back. "You'd better get going. The Joy Boys will be roaming the streets pretty soon. The Mohawks and the Hellfire Club—you know what they do to work addicts."

"Yes sir." The Hand shoved the paper in his pocket and headed for the beltline station.

Cary watched him go—the stick tapping faster now, the tiny screen like a small pillar of fire leading the man on—and felt a new resentment.

He was not on principle a hater of what had come to be called "work addicts" by responsible citymen; nor was he a flagwaver—he never bothered to think of the abortive insurrection when the Hands had revolted, demanding the right to work and an end to the dormitory life to which, for nearly a century, they had been confined like drones. The revolution had been smothered in its own blood and after that there had been a rush of illegal pioneering from the cities to the Unoccupied Country, that almost unpopulated and savage area between the city-strips of the two coasts. Then the migration had to be stamped out, since the system needed a large body of consumers. Finally, in order to head off another revolution it was decided to allow the Hands enough occasional work to syphon off some of their discontent.

It was a wise policy, Cary knew—he did not, like the Joy Boys who had never read Veblen and knew nothing of the problems of a conspicuous consumption economy and who only talked rather vaguely of Wholly Using (like *Holy Dying*, Cary suddenly thought; now where did *that* come in? I'm becoming a living libary of forbidden books)—he did not condemn the Engineers who had made the law allowing the Hands a certain amount of work. No, that was smart Political Engineering. But what did disturb him was that there was, certainly, implied sedition in working. It was, in its way, a criticism of the Political Corporation. But one that must be allowed. It was a disturbing paradox.

He found that, without thinking, he had started through the park. The flowers had just been freshly painted, and they gleamed—pale pastels and brilliant primaries—under the lights. The leaves had been changed too, on the tin trees, and the Autumn set rustled crisply in the wind.

But Nature did not satisfy. The chrome lilies creaked a bit in the light breeze, the mechanical squirrels tirelessly gathered the plastic acorns, the wild dry cataract of light that was the fountain leaped in neonic glory, but there was no water to bless or make fertile.

Now in the deep evening the caretakers appeared to close the flowers and shut off the squirrels. One of them climbed into a tree close to the bench Cary sat on and immediately the sound of birdsong rang down from the metal branches. A nightingale, Cary thought with pleasure; but he was not sure: it might have been a mockingbird or even, he thought, trying to remember the names, a nightjar.

The workless stiffs were filling the tiny park now, the semi-outlaws who refused to become Hands and who managed a marginal existence, working in summer on the few luxury-product farms where work was still permitted, hunting for winter food in the mountains. Bearded and shabby, each with his bindle on his back, they took places under the trees and spread their blankets for the night. Here and there a Sterno lamp glowed into life, and Cary smelled chickory and barley tea being boiled. Somewhere a harmonica began; the dark longing of a blues drifted on the night air, a forbidden tune; but the Beaters did not appear since the park *was* the freedom which the Constitution guaranteed.

Rather drink muddy water, sleep in a hollow log— sharp and impersonal as pain the song cut into Cary's reverie. He was clenched in a long moment of unbearable nostalgia in which the blues, the smell of the coffee, seemed charged with the terrible meaningfulness of

41

dreams, and the intolerable birdsong—nightingale or mockingbird—fell like the slow drops of Chinese water torture. An awful wish (to go home? to be a child? to be free?) grew inside him like one of the metal trees; he felt it grow and blossom inside him, a big bush of pain, cutting and hurting. But at the same time there was a kind of contentment.

Then the harmonica was silent: he heard only the crazy song of the mechanical bird: and he shook his head impatiently and started out of the park.

On the other side there was the inevitable soap-boxer. An old man, this one, with a ragged nimbus of hair and the crazy eyes of a prophet, he shook a long stick at the crowd of listeners.

"—who is God of this world!" the speaker was saying. "Yes, I know there are grumblers among you, men of no faith. Unwilling to admit their guilt, they sleep under the tin trees but sleep lightly, rising early and leaving the city by little-used streets, following the birds to the north or the south in the swing of the seasons, each with a book hidden away somewhere in a hollow tree or behind the embankments of a bridge at a dry river, hiding in their heads a forbidden song or the scrap of an old story. Oh yes, I know them well, for haven't I in my inward and guilty youth, walked the City with my secrets loud in my head, groaning and turning the fiery wheel through the hundred lost seasons of the mortal wish? For I have been as lost as any of you now.

"All roads lead to Rome and all roads lead to the city of the damned. You may enter by the gate of the North, the cold gate of the terrorless and homeless intellect;

42

or through the hot south gate of lust; or through the irresponsible and dreamy eastern gate of the ego, or through the western gate with its dream of human perfection—even this last gate, which is the water gate of birth, the gate of the ocean where everything known or to be known has its twin and counterpart (gate we do not have thought our city is built at the edge of the sea) even this gate is the gate of vanity and sin.

"And how could it be otherwise? For if One were to enter the City sinless, to live a blameless life, would we not all be foul beside him? I have called for water from the dry fountain—is that not blasphemy? But I have been given Light. The accuser who is God of this world is not so unkind as to show us a man who is good. He has given us understanding instead.

"For is it not true that all action is guilt? To sing is vanity; to think is guilt and sin. And this is true because all action is tainted and impure. Did not this God create a world, and was it not a vanity, and did it not bring with it Judgment and that Lucifer, the Devil, who is God's judge? Yea, it was a wise God, for He saw His guilt and created the Devil to be His punisher, just as we have been granted the Investigators and the Beaters and the Legal Engineering to be ours, to juice us, to burn us."

The preacher lifted his hand in gesture toward the flaming spire of Amalgamated Joy. "What is our image of judgment but the consuming fire?"

There were many listeners now, and the soap-boxer lifted his head and continued speaking. His eyes—he was not wearing goggles—burned with his conviction

43

and it seemed to Cary that the man was speaking directly at him.

"Give up the vanities of wish and action, brothers. Put them away with the songs that are better forgotten, the letters better burned, the whores we tupped in the knocking house of our youth. For the great judgment is coming—and the Accuser. I see him now: the iron outriders, the Furies chained to wheels of fire while the great beaked bird screams in the wild heaven. Yes, and the rivers running in blood, the ice wall moving down from the barren mountains in the time when every love is false and every dream a nightmare. Oh hear! That monstrous bird screams in the cold night wind! He is coming! The Accuser! The Accuser who is God of this world!"

The bony finger of the crazy old man pointed off into the darkness over Cary's shoulder. Then Cary saw the bulge of prophecy leave the eyes of the man and sudden apprehension come into them, and involuntarily he turned his head.

It was the Beaters. Cary heard their happy, childish laughter as they came out of the darkness of the park and fell on the ring of listeners, their polished pick-handles flashing in the corner light. The pick-handles rose and fell, a regular, thudding sound as they smashed against flesh, heavier than the screams and groans of the men and the laughter of the Beaters themselves. Cary found himself shouting, wrestling with one of the Beaters, trying to tear the pick-handle from the man's grasp. The Beater laughed, ripped the club away, and started to swing. Then he recognized the Investigator and his face got sulky and he dropped the pick-handle.

44

"You don't want us to have any fun," he said sullenly.

Cary snatched the whistle from the man's belt and blew a long blast. The beating stopped. The listeners had run, most of them, except for a dozen or more who lay on the ground, groaning and trying to drag themselves away. Three Beaters lay on the pavement also, one with his throat neatly cut. The others stood around, grinning and laughing.

"Who's in charge here?"

"Me." It was the man whose club Cary had wrestled for.

"What's the meaning of this? You know free-speech is allowed in the park!"

"Ah, we give them a roust now and then. They get too snotty if we don't."

"It's a violation of your orders!"

"Oh yeah, but who cares?" The Beater grinned and the others broke into laughter.

"Our job's to beat," one of them said seriously.

Christ, thought Cary, what can you do with these morons? "You'd better take care of that fellow," he said, pointing to the Beater whose throat had been cut. The last of the bindle stiffs who had been listening to the soapboxer had crawled away. The old man, too, was gone.

One of the Beaters nudged the man on the ground with his toe. The nearly severed head flopped to one side and the Beaters howled with laughter.

"*Damn* it," Cary said, "if you wanted to do something, why didn't you arrest the old man?"

"Not guilty," the chief Beater said. "He's always

comin' in and confessin' something new. Made up things. Comes in every day. Besides, he's the best speaker. He gets the biggest crowds, like tonight, and that's when we get our kicks. See?"

Cary said nothing. He turned away and walked out of the park, hearing behind him the shouted laughter of the Beaters hauling away their dead.

It had been a rotten day. He went directly now to the car creche and got his vehicle and led it from among the crowded machines, holding the reins at the end of the long snaky neck of the power-pickup. Once outside the creche he put the neck down over the power-filament which was inlaid in the street, felt the field catch, a foot above the asphalt, the neck straight out now as if drinking from an invisible stream. Then he got into the car, set it for automatic, and leaned back. It was a long hour to his house in the suburb of San Francisco.

Sitting relaxed, a tide of images from the activities of the day washed over him and he saw again the verniered dials of the time file, felt again the absolute cold of time in his bones. Who had booby trapped the gadget? Gannell? He had no special reason to suspect Gannell: it was only that on principle Cary suspected everyone and Gannell was closest to hand. It would have been easier for Gannel to get into the office than for anyone else. What did he know about the man?

Nothing very much. Cynicism. Gannell was in charge of the technical end of Investigation Engineering for all of the three states of Los Angeles—a job requiring high responsibility, almost as great responsibility as Cary's own job. Cynicism? It was something to remember.

But, on the other hand, Gannell was stupid—highly competent in his job of course, but still rather stupid, rather unimaginative, hardly the kind of man who could dream of a different kind of society, hardly likely then to risk his neck for one. Still, cynical. And ambitious. Could Gannell, perhaps, be jealous of Cary's own success? Could he be interested in getting Cary's job? Or could there, Cary wondered, be an organization bigger, more far-reaching than he had ever supposed, more dangerous than the petty sedition of the Suspect, the constant opposition of the Hands, the sabotage of men like his brother?

Cary tried to think of his brother now in pure objectivity, as a thing. It was a technique he had learned during his training in Sleuth Engineering—a necessary technique for an Investigator, since in considering the Suspect or Victim as an object, the Investigator was freed from any human responsibility toward him. It allowed the Investigator to establish workable human equations by dropping out of calculation the one awful variable: humanity itself.

Still, Cary could not suppress a certain amount of anger that it should be his own brother—although a brother whom he had not seen for years, had no regard for, had thought, in fact, to be dead—who was upsetting the orderliness of Cary's world. Damn him, Cary thought; *who* would have supposed that one's own brother. . . .

Far ahead something flickered onto the highway, almost empty now in the approach to San Luis. For an instant he felt the leap of fear and then recognized what it was. Without thinking he flicked the drive switch to

47

manual and turned the car out of the lane. The thing ahead was caught, crucified in the stream of pitiless light for a fraction of a second that was too long. It tried to dodge, Cary swerved the car slightly, saw the thing loom bigger in his light, felt the thump and splatter, the matchstick crackle of bone as they hit. The car lurched and skidded and then he had it under control again. He moved back into his lane, switched to automatic and saw the snaky neck of the pickup dream once more toward the copper filament.

Sitting back, he felt a sudden tiredness like a disease and thought of the Suspect, of Gannell, of his brother. The nausea climbing toward his throat brought with it an image of the flowers and then one of his wife. Everybody, *everybody* must be suspected.

He was sorry now for the rabbit he had hit. As the car slowed, beginning its long approach to the suburb of San Francisco, he flashed on the spellcast and his nausea gradually disappeared. With his arms crossed over his chest he hardly noticed that he was shivering.

II.

"And now," the Omnivoice was saying, "we bring you what was once called the 'national anthem' of a primitive tribe known as the 'Irish.' It is called 'The Irish Black Bottom' (in recognition, one supposes, of either a tribal characteristic or a taboo of some sort) and it is a representative work of a type called 'jass.'"

Lulubel stood in front of her mirror covering her slick, sensuous and unrepentant flesh with a small fireworks of black and gold sequins. She hummed to herself, a nameless tune, while the Omnivoice like a mothering and pentecostal pure snow of sound fell out of the ceiling and walls. Dancing to the slow rhythm of the imaginary tune, she turned her backside to the mirror, gave her buttocks three fictive and narcissistic pats, and surveyed the result like a retired and literary general gazing at an old battlefield and imagining the deployment of forces in past and legendary skirmishes.

In partes tres, Lulubel hummed, admiring the generous provinces of her fundament and thinking of the words of a song from the most recent Opera Engineering review; *ars est celare artem.* And turned herself and her attention to the proliferent blonde and immemorial bush, the badge and beaver of her April womanhood.

"This particular 'record' was discovered recently by our Historical Engineers and has not yet been placed on

49

the Index," the ceiling cooed. "Therefore you may listen without trepidation, O happy Angelinos of the suburb of San Francisco! The work is being played by a group of primitive Music Engineers led by Turkish Murphy, one of the poets of this suburb in those dark and unhappy times."

Lulubel put a small torch of paint to her belly and looked at herself in the mirror. Blank, visionary, like the flower in the heart of the lotus, the eye gazed serenely out of her navel. Satisfied, winking once at the eye, she picked up another brush and drew a slashing arrow of black across her left flank. Real skitz, she told herself, looking at it critically; and drew a yellow curving arrow up her right forward leg. Militant as the arrows on a military map, the signs suggested a battle of encirclement. She looked at it and it was good.

Next she put on a pair of high black stockings and then the glass slippers with the six-inch heels. Finally, the dress, a gossamer sheath, a kind of conspiracy of mist. She looked at herself in the mirror, while a wild rain of beautiful and strange and disturbing music fell from the ceiling. Under the film of the dress her body glowed like a moon in a light wash of cloud, the sequins glittered and winked, the strategic arrows pointed.

"Not bad," she sighed, and was suddenly bored with it, with the new creations of the Style Engineers, and she felt that her feet hurt.

"Maybe he'll like it," she said aloud. "Maybe it's worth it to dress up."

And went out of the room and got herself a drink and went away from the music which filled her with its dreams and thunder and across the small back yard, perfectly mechanized and bright with chrome but with one semi-illegal geranium blooming in a corner, to where Sy Levin sprawled in a long chair under a soft light. Who looked up at her then, whistling.

"*Mighty* pretty," he said. He stood up, tall, thin, handsome, and looked at her stars and arrows. "The map of love," he said.

"What?"

"The way you look," he said. "The arrows and the rest of it. It's a quotation from an old poet."

"Oh," she said. "That." And sat down across from him.

"You really are very pretty."

"I suppose so." She sighed. "It's a nuisance getting dressed up like this. But it's Club night. And anyway . . . I guess I'd rather be happy than pretty."

Levin looked at her in surprise. "It's your *duty* to be happy," he said.

"I know," Lulubel said. "It's such a bore."

"Strange talk for a joygirl."

"But that's just it. I'm not a joygirl any more. I'm a wife. I'm *supposed* to be a wife. But what does that mean? It's supposed to mean something, isn't it?"

"It used to."

"Yes, but what? I thought it'd be—oh, I don't know. Hard, maybe. Difficult, like something you like to do that takes practice, but that you like to do *because* it's hard. Sy, did you ever ski?"

"Yes."

"Should be like skiing, I guess."

51

"Maybe this is part of it. Right now, I mean, this upsetness of yours—maybe that's part of the difficulty you expected."

"Oh." She thought about it and made a face. "Can't be," she said. "You got anything to drink? Maybe I'll get drunk. You want to get drunk, Sy?"

"I *am* drunk," he said. "But I suppose we should drink some more. It's Club night."

"Where's Clarabel?" she asked.

"Getting dressed. No—here she is now."

A tall redheaded girl in high boots and a handful of beads came out of the house.

"Hi, Lulubel," she said. "All set?" She put the tray she was carrying on a table beside the chairs. "You want a drink?"

"Sure."

"You're certainly undressed up," Sy told her.

"For you, my dear husband. Like it?"

She pirouetted slowly and he slapped the round uncovered buttock.

She squealed: "Ah, daddio! We're gonna break the bank tonight!"

"Pour us a drink," Sy said.

"I wish Johnny would get here," Lulubel said.

"How is he these days?" Sy asked her. "I never see him."

"Busy. Too busy. I hardly see him either. Half the time he doesn't come home—stays in the city and works. And when he does come home he's beat."

"Take him on a vacation," Clarabel said. "All work and no play, you know."

"He won't go."

"Then take one yourself."

"Clarabel's Law," Sy said. "Take a drink or take a vacation." He handed his empty glass back for a refill and picked up the pad from the table beside his arm.

"What were you doing when I came over, Sy?"

"Writing," he said. He held up the pad. "You do it this way." He fished a pencil out of his pocket and made marks on the paper.

"I thought they had writing machines for everything?"

"They do. For spellcasts and all of that. But I got a pass to the library the other day—it's one of the privileges you get if you're a writer. And it reminded me that this was how they did it in the past. Thought I'd like to try it."

"Is it fun?"

"It's hard. You have to *think* of everything and then you have to write it down. No machines to take your feeling and make a story out of it, or take your story and incorporate feeling in it. You have to do it all by yourself."

"*That's* my clever husband," Clarabel said. "Does everything the hard way. Besides, it's probably illegal. It's more than twenty-one years old, isn't it?"

"Yes, it's many centuries old," Sy said. "But it's not strictly illegal. Anyway, Lu won't turn me in."

"Sure I will," Lulubel said. "When John gets home I'll——" Then she saw that he wasn't joking. "Sy——"

"I know you wouldn't," he said, patting the black net stocking. "I know you wouldn't."

"John wouldn't do anything like——"

"Of course not."

"You have your hand on my best friend's best leg," Clarabel said. "What next?"

"More drinks," Sy told her.

"What did you write?" Lulubel asked him. She held out her glass. She wanted to be drunk now. She didn't want to think of what he had said.

"Only got one line all afternoon," Sy told her. "Something I remembered from one of the old books. I was trying to see what might go with it. It was a kind of a poem, but I can't remember the rest of it."

"What is it?"

"*Mary had a little lamb.* I can't remember what comes next. A rhyme or something. I've been trying to figure out what."

"Sure," Clarabel said. "Mary had a little lamb, and then she had a little drink. Want a drink?"

"Thanks," Lulubel said. "It must be nice to be a writer."

She picked up the drink and heard, across the narrow back yard, the sound of the phone in her own house. She put down the drink and ran across the lighted space.

Sy watched her, a starry cloud of flesh, running.

"Mighty nice stuff," he said.

"Mighty nice stuff right here," Clarabel said. "You want that, Sy?"

Levin flicked her beads as if working an abacus. "That's not what I meant," he said.

"That's not what I meant either. Just remember that he *is* an Investigator. This may be the Home and the

King's Ex and all that, but just remember."

In a moment they watched Lulubel come across the lawn toward them.

"That's funny," she said.

"What?"

"I thought it was Johnny. It sounded like him. But it was his *brother*."

"Didn't know he had one," Sy said.

"Yes. But I thought he was dead. It's very odd." She shook her head puzzledly.

"Have a drink," Clarabel said.

Lulubel drank it as a gulp and then they all heard it —the high whining signal of the autocar opening its stall beside the house.

"Johnny's home!" Lulubel cried. She jumped up and started across the lawn. Then she came back and poured herself another drink and drank it quickly. "See you tonight," she said, and ran toward her house.

"Home is the hunter," Sy said. He and Clarabel watched the firefly signals of Lulubel's sequins as she ran across the grass.

————o————

Cary turned in at his house and his machine let out its mechanical bleat and the door of the stall slid open. He put the long snake-head of the apparatus into the atomic feedbag to replenish the power reservoirs for manual control and waited a moment before going into the house.

Now that he was here he felt better. The Home,

the King's Ex, allowed only to the highest state functionaries or to the very rich, was inviolate, and every time he returned he sensed a kind of release in himself, a feeling of security. He waited for it now, hearing the soft sibilant drinking sounds of the machine, but it didn't come.

In the soft early night he heard the sound of a mechanical bird and from the loudspeaker on the corner came the rustle of trees and the papery music of crickets —all sounds he had subscribed to and paid for—but tonight they did not soothe. He hoped that Lulubel was with one of her friends, Clarabel, Annabel, Maybel, Mirabel—he didn't care. He wanted to be alone. He wanted, he knew now, to sleep for a week. He put his hand to the plate and the door swung open and he went into his house.

"Daddio!"

"You're drunk," he said, and braced himself, feeling smothered in her embrace.

"Of course I'm drunk," she said and kissed him again hard on the mouth. "Aren't all good Users drunk after sunset? And it's Club night, too."

Cary groaned and let himself be led to a chair, let her take off his shoes, his travel clothes; let her put a drink in his hand.

"Hiroshima," she toasted him, and lifted her own glass.

Cary drank dutifully, feeling a far-off tremor inside himself, a submarine explosion. The eye of Lulubel's navel, blank, impassive, gazed at him, a visionary and magical ship adrift on the lake of her belly. The drink was already having its effect. He winked solemnly at the eye and Lulubel came across the room to him and sat in his lap. He felt her hand move across the bare flesh of his back.

"Punch my ticket, Daddio?"

"Damn it, Lu, I just got home!"

"Be nice, Daddio!"

"Later," he said, and pushed her off his lap and stood up. "Later. We're running on credit anyway."

"Not any more, we're not," Lulubel said. "Besides, love's fun, isn't it?"

"There is a time for all things," Cary said. Something nagged his memory. "What do you mean we're not on credit?"

"Look at the bank if you don't believe me."

He went across to the Reichsbank. The machine, named for some forgotten authority on the orgasm, stood near the entrance door. There was a long-handled lever on the right side of it, two identifier plates for thumb-prints labeled HIS and HERS, and, behind glass at the front, a series of wheels with phalli painted on them. At the top there were two smaller glassed-in areas marked SCORE. Beside it was the calendar date and the time. 7:23 PM, Cary noted automatically. Both score sheets were blank.

"I don't understand it," he said.

"What, Johnny?"

"But we *had* credit!"

"Sure, last week. But time goes by, you know. We didn't have credit enough to last a whole week."

"But damn it, just last night——"

57

"What do you mean? You weren't home last night."

"Not home!" For a moment he felt as he had when the time-file had gone wrong: an invisible garrot tightened on his throat; he tasted his own fear.

He sat down and took the new drink she held out to him.

"Not home!"

"For the last two nights. Why? What's the matter?"

"I'd forgotten."

"Forgotten? Baby, you *are* working too hard. And I'm lonely. I don't *like* to have you stay in town to work all the time."

"Not much longer," he said automatically. "Was I gone last week too?"

"Couple of nights. Tuesday, I think, or Wednesday. And Friday. Don't you remember?"

"I guess so. Yes, I remember now."

But he did not remember.

"You're working too hard," Lulubel said.

"Yes. I'd better get dressed I suppose. Club Night —we've got to go out."

"Yes. Sure you don't want any action now, baby?"

"No," he said, too tired to resent it. And went across toward the sleeping room.

"Oh. I forgot. Your brother called."

"Brother?"

"Yeah. He said he was your brother. I was surprised. I didn't know you *had* a brother, still alive, I mean."

"I don't. I don't recognize him as a brother. When did he call?"

"Just a few minutes before you came."

"You're drunk," he said flatly. "*I* called you."

"Johnny, you're crazy!"

"I called you on my way home. I thought I did. What did he say?"

"Just asked when you would be home. What is it? Is something wrong?"

"No," he said tiredly. "Nothing. They just won't let me alone."

"Who won't?"

"Never mind. I'm worn out I guess. I forget things. The other day I bought some flowers. I forgot about that too."

"Why don't you try the Psychomat?"

"You know I hate that damned thing!"

"Johnny!"

For half a minute and with hardly any surprise at all, he heard himself screaming obscenities at her, saw the shock and—what was it? loathing, hatred? pity?: he felt a deep and buried thrill of satisfaction—on her face. Then he stopped.

"Sorry, Lu," he said in a choked voice. He felt sick with something—shame? guilt?—which was unknown and meaningful as an image from a nightmare. "I guess I *should* use the Psychomat. Didn't know your husband could be seditious, did you?" he tried to joke. "Or such a bastard?"

"It's all right."

For a moment he thought she was going to cry and he turned away toward the sleeping room.

The door of the Psychomat had the usual controls and he set them now from *automatic* to *manual* because

59

he did not want to be groggy from the truth sedative. He had never used it much anyway: there was something frightening in the thought.

He went inside and the blue lamp went on: the couch was a small island in a sea of artificial moonlight. He lay down on it now and curled himself into a foetal position. "Bless me, father," he said, and went mechanically through the ritual of the beginning. "When I was a boy," he said, and heard the glib and often repeated words rattle like pebbles on the walls of the tiny room. He watched the blank and moony dial-face of the machine, feeling some of the tension leaving him.

"And what about your brother?"

For a moment he was too shocked to believe that it was the machine which had spoken.

"Nothing," he said, finally.

"Then why did you mention him?"

"I didn't!"

"Excuse me," the machine said. "Would you like to listen to a playback of the tape?"

"No! I mean—what has my brother to do with this?"

"Excuse me. That is what I must find out."

"It is a state secret."

"Excuse me. One has no secrets from one's Confessomech."

"I'm ending the ssesion," Cary said. He sat up on the couch. "I am heartily sorry," he intoned, beginning the Act of Contrition.

"Excuse me," the machine said. "But you are not."

Cary heard the faint click, and in the luminous darkness of the room he saw the snaky tentacle come out

60

of the wall. He leaped away from the couch, but the walls seemed to have moved closer, the room was too small, there was no place to run to.

"Excuse me. This will only take a second. It will not hurt."

"Stop it," he shouted. "Stop!" And began to scream, knowing in a part of his mind, that the room was totally soundproof. Like a man crucified, he hung against the wall and watched the blind snaky head of the tentacle search for him. Then he ripped off one of his slippers and struck out.

The head pulled back, as if puzzled, and then hunted for him again, moving across the couch where he had been lying.

"Excuse me," the machine said. "This is for your own good. I am forced——"

With all his might Cary flung the slipper at the milky dial face. Glass broke, the blue overhead light went out, in the blackness he heard a faint mechanical sigh, a distant and dying, hollow, light, crystalline ticking, like the beating of a glass heart. In the deathly quiet and absolute night of the closet, Cary heard the rasp and thump of the tentacle-head as it searched for him. Then, later, nothing at all.

After a while, shaking, he found his pencil flash and turned it on. In the narrow beam, Cary saw the tentacle. It rested on the floor. The long flat jaws were open and the fangs of the hypo needles glittered. The machine was dead and the tentacle was lifeless now, and Cary picked up his slipper and, in a galvanic spasm of rage and terror, as if he were killing a snake, he struck at the

61

lifeless mechanism, pounding it into the floor, smashing it apart. Then he began to vomit.

Sitting on the couch, the sickness momentarily over, he tried to make the trembling go away. Why had the machine gone crazy this way? It would not have run amuck if left to itself. *Who*, he asked himself desperately, remembering the time-file. *Who?* Someone had fixed the machine—*who?* He thought of all the people he knew, ending with Levin who lived across the yard, and thought of them all in a flash of electric hatred. But *why?* Not Levin, he thought, forcing himself to look at the writer coldly, as a thing. Unlikely, anyway, unless Levin were part of the conspiracy. Gannell? He had been out to visit them last week. His brother? There was nothing to tell him anything. His mind working automatically now, he thought of all of them and put them away for lack of evidence. Lulubel? A good, stupid, pretty, expensive, decorous wife, a retired "belle" of the Joygirls, she seemed to him happily incapable of thinking at all. *Who then?*

All of us are born with it, he thought; everyone is suspect.

The enormity of it was crushing. He saw sedition streaming through time and the firmament like the billion tiny flares of starlight.

Who will help me? he asked himself in mortal anguish. *Who will help me?*

But in the dark night of the Psychomat and of the soul there was nothing to answer him.

———o———

"Let's not go into the Obscenity Room," Clarabel said. "It's simply too *bourgeois.*"

They were at the Alcatraz Club across the bay and it was now almost midnight.

"I don't care where we sit," Cary said wearily. "But let's sit. I'm a tired man."

"Let's go into the Game Room," Lulubel said. "You like that, don't you?" They went into the Game Room.

It was as big as an amphitheatre and where the upward slope of the bowl began there was a track for the drag races. One was in progress as they went in—the kiddie-kars whirled on the track in a high whine of metal. Walking toward a table at the center of the room, Cary tensed himself, waiting for the inevitable crack-up. He had never got used to it.

"I suppose when the old boys invented the cyclotron they couldn't have known it'd be adapted for drag races," Levin said.

"No." Cary did not want to encourage one of Levin's literary conversations.

"Or else they'd have worked out a way to reduce the noise," Levin said, wincing as the whine increased in volume.

They saw the cars bunch on the turn, stream out into the straightaway, bunch again. There was a sudden ripping sound, the crunch of plastic and glass, and then two quick butcher-shop thumps and the wall splashed into red. The kiddie-cars whined into the straightaway and ground to a stop.

"Well, that's over anyway," Clarabel sighed. "Drinks, everybody?"

63

"I suppose so," Cary said. He wanted desperately to be drunk, but now, with the liquor from the earlier part of the evening souring in his belly, he was afraid he couldn't be. He put his hand on the space-warp servitor and a bar bloomed at his elbow. He could not get the first drink past his nose.

"Don't drink it if you don't want it, Johnny," Lulubel said. "We'll take care of your quota."

The solicitude in her eyes angered him. He saw Levin carefully looking the other way. "I can take care of my own responsibilities," he said icily. "Just attend to your own."

"Here, daddio," Clarabel said. "You don't have to drink that stuff. Want some pop?"

She waved her hand and a tall blonde in a topless, backless, frontless and bottomless dress came toward their table. The woman carried a small tray suspended by silver straps from her neck. On the box Cary saw the syringes and the pipes, the little brown pellets and the white powder.

"No," he said.

"Go on, it's fun." Clarabel gestured at the tray.

"This is real crazy shit," the blonde said drowsily.

"You want some Horse, daddio?" Clarabel asked him. "You want to kick it around a little?"

"I got some pot, too," the blonde said. "And yen pok."

"No," Clarabel said. "This has got to be *fast*." She reached out and began to roll up Cary's sleeve. Levin watched them curiously. Cary could feel the tension in Lulubel, her anxiety for him.

"Oh for God's sake!" he said. "Anything!" And he watched the blonde light a small lamp on the tray, take out a syringe, pick up some of the white powder. He hunted in his pocket for money.

"No," Clarabel said. "Let me straighten you. It's my party." She put a bill on the tray.

"Want to get stoned?" the blonde asked politely. "Or you just want to get high?"

"He doesn't want to be blind," Clarabel said primly.

The blonde put a strap on his arm; he felt dizziness as the circulation cut off, then the prick of the needle in his vein.

"Kick it!" Clarabel said. "Boot it!"

He had a momentary feeling that it had started to snow and then he felt relaxed and at ease.

———o———

Club night was an institution. No one knew quite how it had got started, although the historians sometimes made vague references to "smokers," whatever they were, and to an old quasi-religious organization called Kiwanis. Club night was not mandatory, but it was now part of "the tradition" and so in some respects was more obligatory than if it had been required by law. Sitting at the center of the Game Room, listening to the chatter of Lulubel and the Levins, Cary felt withdrawn, tolerant, amused. For the first time, under the cloudy influence of the drug, he was enjoying what before he had regarded as a duty. Then the cloud darkened; something —a memory? something he had forgotten to do?— nagged at him.

65

"Listen," he said suddenly to Levin. "You ever had any trouble with your Psychomat?"

"Trouble?" Levin lifted a quizzical eyebrow.

"Trouble!" Clarabel hooted. "He drove it nuts. It got so neurotic it simply couldn't function. We had to get it *analyzed.*"

"Expensive, too," Levin said, nodding, making rings with his drink. "Costs a lot to have one sent to a machine-shrinker."

"What is it, Johnny?" Lulubel asked. "Did something happen?" Again he saw the shadow of anxiety—or was it fear?—in her eyes; and it angered him.

"Forget it," he said curtly.

"You sure come down fast, daddio," Clarabel told him. "You want another fix?"

"I don't want anything."

"Mr. Cary?"

"Yes?" He looked at the Joy Girl who had come up to their table.

"You're wanted in the Assignation Parlor at once."

"Ooh!" squealed Clarabel. "Romance! Somebody's on the make for you."

"I have no intention of going."

Cary had always inwardly disapproved of the Assignation Parlors and the ritual of promiscuity. Now he felt vaguely embarrassed and harassed.

"And leave some poor girl in pain all night? That's not the gentlemanly thing to do," Clarabel told him. "You go and put money in her bank."

"He'd better think of putting money in his *own* bank first!" Lulubel said hotly.

Cary looked at her in surprise, at the anger and the hurt in her eyes. She's going to cry, he told himself in wonder; and felt a warming thrill of power.

"It's a man," the Joy Girl said.

"Gannell," Cary said immediately. "He probably figured I'd be here and wanted to talk to me about something."

He got up abruptly, feeling at ease and certain once more, on the firm ground of professional routine. He felt sorry for his wife now, and said, kindly, "Excuse me, Lu," and followed the girl across the huge room to the Parlors.

A Joy Girl standing under the insignia and slogan (We Satisfy) of her organization asked mechanically, "Punch my ticket, daddio?" but Cary did not answer, going on through the aphrodisiacal perfume and the knowing laughter of the sexual ancient whispering dark toward the cubicle to which he had been directed.

No one was in the tiny room, but he was not surprised —he had not expected Gannell in person. He sat down on the bed which was the only piece of furniture and turned on the audio.

At first there was no sound, then only a whisper. He thought, with shock and resentment, that it was not Gannell after all, that some woman, as was commonly done, was propositioning him without wanting to reveal herself. A prude or a pervert, he thought; one who likes to hide. He turned up the audio to full volume.

It did not help. The voice continued in a feverish whisper, only a little louder now. To Cary, sitting in the deep artificial dusk of the little room, it sounded

67

crazy, wild, full of hate. He leaned closer, trying to make out the words and then he got it—a long endless sigh of obscenity ending with a choked *I'll kill you, I'll kill you.* Then the obscenity again and the threat, and Cary heard himself shouting *Who are you?* but there was no answer except the steady mad whispering flow of obscenity and threat, the blur of an image on the screen where whoever it was had blanked out the televisor to conceal his identity. Cary flipped off the audio switch.

He sat there for a long time, sweating and shaken and trying to think. There had been a terrible familiarity about the voice, even though it had spoken only in a whisper. His brother? He knew that he was grasping at the obvious and he forced himself to consider other possibilities. They were limited enough. Working as he did behind a screen of secrecy, there were few people who were close to him, who knew him, who might want him out of the way. Gannell—the ambitious man. Then, remembering the Psychomat's behavior, he thought of Lulubel. Of the Levins.

But why should they want him *dead?* He was accustomed to sedition and conspiracy, as well as to the cynicisms and deviations of his wife, acquaintances and friends—even of himself. But the shocking brutality of the voice was beyond that—it had been full of an awful hate, a desire to destroy him. Once more he went around the terrible circle of those he must suspect, adding now the Umpire with whom he had once had trouble, adding the pitiful Stoolpigeon of the afternoon session, immediately dismissing them both.

He was back again to his brother, that monstrous familiarity of voice, recognizable and strange as his own voice in dreams, and he felt again the anger and frustration he had experienced on his drive home. The irrationality and utter disorderliness of the whole thing offended him. If people had to be seditious, let them do their job and he would do his job, which was to catch and punish them. There was no reason to be personal about it.

But he would have to be personal. He would have to catch or kill someone or be killed himself. Put that way it seemed momentarily simple and he went back to the table in the big room.

"Nice?" Clarabel leered at him.

"Was it Gannell?"

"No, Lu." He saw the anger—jealousy? again he felt surprise; he had never thought of anyone as capable of being jealous of him—as it came into her eyes. "Business," he said. "About the job I'm on now."

"Something new?" Clarabel asked.

No one said anything. Levin carefully looked away from his wife as if interested in the new drag race that was just starting.

"Did it again," Clarabel said brightly. "Always talking out of turn. Come on Lu, let's go watch the Russian roulette. The finalist survivor is here tonight and he's going to try the five-to-one shot. Have you seen him? M-m-m! He's one of the Hands—but good looking? Oh, daddio! They say if he wins he's asking for citizenship instead of the prize. But he won't win, of course. Come on, baby."

Cary watched them walk away and turned abruptly to Levin.

"What about the Psychomat?"

"Well, what about it?"

"Did yours break down?"

"Oh, that." Levin got himself another drink and leaned back in his chair. "Yes, it broke down, just as Claire told you. Went neurotic. Made me very happy."

"It didn't—well—attack you? Try to sedate you by force?"

"No. What are you getting at, old man?" Levin appeared sober enough now. He looked at Cary sharply.

"Have you ever heard of one doing that?"

"I think so," Levin said slowly. "In special circumstances. If the Psycho thought it was required."

"I've never heard of a machine doing that," Cary said. "I wondered if someone had been tinkering with it. As a joke, maybe."

"It wouldn't be a very pleasant joke," Levin said. "Of course the things do foul up every once in a while. The small victories of our time."

"What do you mean?"

"Haven't you ever noticed how everyone is happy when a complicated machine breaks down? Or when someone stops acting like a machine and acts like a real human being?"

"I don't understand you," Cary said. He had discovered that he was capable of drinking alcohol again and was into his second drink. The liquor coupled with his exhaustion made him feel relaxed, drowsy, and the noises of the game room were distant and unreal.

"We live in a machine society," Levin went on. "We've carried its use nearly to the ultimate. We've used it to

70

conquer space and even to some degree, time, and we've built up an economy where everything is done for us, even most of our thinking and some of our feeling, by machines or machine-like men. But basically man doesn't want to be a machine. He wants to be a man, whatever *that* is. So when a machine fouls up it always makes us happy, we exult in secret, because it leaves a momentary loophole for our humanity. *We* make mistakes, so when the machine makes one we say: 'Ah ha! It's weak like us.' It makes us think, at least for the time, that we're superior to the machine, instead of subordinate to it."

"But we *should* be subordinate to it. Don't the Sociological Engineers have an axiom: 'Man is an appendage to the machine'?"

"Sure they have, but nobody likes it that way!"

"Don't you?"

"John," Levin said. "We've known each other for a long time and we've been friendly. But that's the kind of question I can't very well answer. You're the Investigator, you know."

"You could answer me as one of your friends."

"In a total machine society, the function replaces the personality. It's impossible to forget, after all, that you *are* the Investigator. No, I won't answer it. This is just talk. I'm explaining what in the old days would be called the philosophy or psychology behind behavior in a machine society. None of this, of course, is my personal belief."

Cary heard the mockery in the voice, but in his alcoholic well-being it did not disturb him. He was not even disturbed by the implied sedition. "Let's just talk

71

then," he said, beginning to feel the afflatus of the neophyte philosopher.

"Talk then," Levin said.

"Where you're wrong, Sy," Cary told him, "is at just this point: man *wants* to be an appendage to the machine. Sort of mechanical apron strings tied to him. That's what he *wants*, and that's what the Political Engineers discovered long ago. He doesn't *want* to be free, to be himself. As you say: *to be himself*—what does that mean anyway? Man is afraid to find out. Maybe he's nothing at all. Or maybe he's something wonderful. What difference would it make? Both would be terrible, because even if he *were* supposed to be something wonderful, how awful it would be to try to become that! No, it's better for him to remain attached to the machine."

"The umbilical cord," Levin said. "But if you're right, why does man resent it so much? Why the need for Investigators and Beaters and the Punishment.Department and all the rest of it? The Spellcasts, Club Night—every institution in society either punishes him when he acts out his resentment or attempts to drain off that resentment before it can lead to action. Isn't that what education is for, and psychomats and alcohol and drugs—even the labor that's allotted to the work addicts? To draw out, or ground or soak up our resentments? I'm just making talk you understand. I'm not really questioning."

"Of course."

"*Why* the resentment against the machine then?"

"Didn't you hate your parents?"

"Listen," Levin said a little stiffly. "I know that all writers are officially classified as nuts, but I had a perfectly normal childhood. *Naturally* I hated by parents."

"There's your answer."

"You mean that the resentment against machines is like our resentment of our parents? But we don't *have* to be dependent on machines. We could be their masters. Besides I'm not convinced that everyone at all times *did* hate their parents. I've seen some of the old books—with permission of course—and I'm not sure that hating one's parents is instinctive and universal."

"You're on the wrong track," Cary said. He was into his third drink and felt wise and benignant. "How'd you feel when you had carried one of your resentments against your parents into action? How'd you feel when you'd been punished?"

"I don't know. I'm not sure I *was* punished."

"Should have been," Cary assured him. "If you *weren't* punished, perhaps that's what made you into a neurotic artist. But I'll tell you how you *should* have felt. If you'd been punished. You *should* have been punished, Sy."

"How should I have felt?"

"Content," Cary said. "You should have felt content." He remembered now, through the fog of whisky, the booby-trapped time-file and that other feeling he had felt mixed in with his fear—contentment. Yes, But, he thought, *I'm* not being punished. There was something wrong, mixed up, in his thinking, he knew; but in the transfiguration of alcohol he could not quite put his finger on it. He was aware that Levin was looking at him as, he imagined, one might look at a foetal monster. "Because you were guilty," Cary said. "You should have felt content because you were guilty and were punished

73

and so you should have felt content."

"But I never *felt* guilty!"

"Should have," Cary said kindly.

"But damn it I WASN'T GUILTY!" Levin bawled.

"That's what *you* think," Cary said smugly.

Owlishly, conspiratorially, he looked at Levin over the rim of his glass. "Everybody's guilty," he said, and sniggered like a boy.

"You too?" Levin asked quietly.

"What would I be guilty of?"

"All right," Levin said. "How could an Investigator be guilty? But now I'll tell you something. I'll 'talk' to you. The only things I *feel* guilty about are the things the Political Corporation pays me and praises me for—the crap I write for the Spellcasts. I'm a *writer*," he said, his voice honey-thick with self-contempt. "You know what a *writer* is—and what he was? I've been looking it up in the library. He *was* a man who told the *truth*. He wanted to see the way things are and put it down that way. And what are writers now but a bunch of liars and pussyfooters—Spellcasters!—trying to be first in bed with the latest fashionable idea? Take Ounce or Blatherwell, or Shaper or Futz—in love with Italian tyrants of the sixteenth and twentieth centuries or with the Middle Ages or with Romish religion or with 'personalism' and all of them mincing or blathering or shaping or futzing about to suit the latest windshift of the Political Corporation. Yes, I *feel* guilty about being part of that daisy chain. Just *feeling* guilty is, of course, actual guilt, even if you haven't *done* anything wrong. I know that. But I don't just *feel* guilty. I really *am* guilty. That gives me a certain comfort. Do you understand?"

Levin was leaning across the table, his eyes blazing.

"This is just talk?" Cary asked.

"Oh sure." Levin slumped back in his chair and picked up his glass. "You don't think I'm crazy enough to be serious, do you? I'm a writer, aren't I? A Spellcaster?"

"I think you're a sick man," Cary told him.

He wondered how much Levin believed of what he had said. Enough. Too much. It was axiomatic that everyone was guilty to one degree or another. The alcohol made his brain sluggish and he could not define for himself the central error of Levin's thinking and it made him angry. "You're crazy," he said. "You're crazy to talk this way, even if it's only talk." He sneered at Levin. "You ought to have your head examined. No wonder your Psychomat went neurotic."

"Consciousness is a disease of matter."

"What do you mean?"

"A philosopher said it," Levin told him. "How do I know what it means? I'm not supposed to think. I'm a writer."

"A disease. A disease of matter. That's very good."

"Is it?"

"It defines the problem."

"Is there a problem?"

"The problem of sedition, of conspiracy," Cary said impatiently. "It has its origin in consciousness, doesn't it?"

"But consciousness has its origin in things. Consciousness it a product of the friction between ourselves and the world."

"Who cares where it comes from? One expression of consciousness in our society is sedition, conspiracy, revolt. Diseased consciousness. That's what I'm thinking of."

"Well, the solution is obvious," Levin said.

"Of course. Reduce consciousness."

Cary picked up his glass and drank thirstily. He had the feeling of being on the verge of understanding something enormously complicated and simple.

"Simple," Levin said. "Have you thought of the greatest possible reduction of consciousness?"

"What do you mean?"

"The perfect state," Levin said. "The perfectly orderly state: death."

Cary felt cheated, as if Levin had made a bad joke. He started to speak.

"Let's drop it," Levin said. "I've got an advanced case of the disease. I'm sick of talking. Want to sober up and go home?"

"I suppose," Cary said automatically. He felt a sudden disappointment, as if a party were ending earlier than he wanted it to, as if some discovery had been denied to him. He looked at the liquor in his glass, wondering if he should drink it. He had been on the verge of something—joy? release?—and he wanted to be drunk, to be drunk and free. But he took the pill that Levin was holding out to him, knowing that it was the sensible thing to do, and swallowed it.

Immediately he was aware of the noise in the game room, the sound of jets and gunfire, the drunken shouts and laughter. He was cold sober and tired.

"What a night," he said. "I must have drunk a lot, my memory's all blurry."

"Mine too," Levin said. "I think we talked a lot. I remember talking a lot of nonsense. Do you remember?"

"A little." Shards of the discussion scratched at his memory—a jigsaw puzzle he did not, at the moment, have the energy to put together. Now that the anti-alcohol pill had made him crashingly sober, Cary felt again the itch and rub of his anxiety, the nag of the old questions. His brother? Gannell? Wearily he went on turning the wheel of his mystery.

"We'd better go," Levin said. "It's almost three o'clock and I've got a spell to cast. I'll go find the girls."

Cary watched him cross the long room. What was it Levin had said? The disease of matter. Consciousness. Let that go. Question of what man wants.

He pushed the fragments of thought out of his mind, watching Levin, trying not to think at all, but it was impossible to stop thinking. As if the ideas had a life of their own they flickered into being in the dark of his mind and he wearily pushed them away again. Gannell? He watched his wife coming across the room toward him, walking carefully as if the floor were a thin and slippery ice, and he remembered again the horrible moment in the psychomat. Her?

"Hello, daddio," Lulubel said. "What'samatter, honey, don't you swing good tonight?"

"It's time we left," he said. "Here." He pushed a pill across the table toward her.

"Do 'wanna get sober!"

"For God's sake Lu, look at the time! I'm knocked out. I want to get home to bed!"

"Bed. Good." She reached for the pill and swallowed it. "Gee," she said, a moment later. "I guess we hung on a good one didn't we? Look at Clarabel!"

Cary watched Levin supporting his wife across the floor. "Let's go," he said. And to Levin: "Meet you out front." And led his wife toward the door.

"Levin been over to our place recently?" he asked.

"No." Lulubel gave him a quick look. "Why?"

"Just wondering," he said, thinking of a snaky neck striking at him in the darkness of a little room.

"If you're wondering about *that*," Lulubel said, "you can stop right now. You know it's all right there in the bank for you."

"Used to be kept in the heart."

"What?"

"That's what they used to say. 'I keep your love in my heart.' I wonder why we changed?"

"Maybe because banks are a safer place to keep it," Lulubel said, yawning. "If love is money."

"Time is money."

"What?"

"Another thing they used to say in the old days. 'Time is money.'"

"You're so smart," Lulubel said, yawning again; and the Levins came out of the club and they all got into the machine and went home.

Cary put the nose of the machine in the atomic feedbag

78

and followed the girls—they had dropped Levin at his office—up the walk toward his front door. He noticed that in spite of the anti-alcohol pill, Clarabel was still weaving.

"It's so cold! Oh, my naked ass!" she moaned softly; and put her purse over her unclothed posterior.

Cary held his thumb against the identifier plate and the door opened and somewhere a bird sang ten clear notes as if piping them aboard.

"Sorry we can't ask you to stay," Lulubel said in a voice of dismissal as they entered.

"I know how it is," Clarabel said. She gave a leer at the Reichsbank and went through the French doors, her behind bobbing—while Cary thought 'shine little glow-worm' and 'lead kindly light' (sourly; wondering where he had come by this cargo of literary contraband; still feeling a little hung over)—and past the quasi-legal geranium from which she plucked the single testimentary, wilted flower.

He began to be aware of an odd scratching sound.

Lulubel was in the sleeping room; he heard the broken-glass sound of her clothing falling, the music box tinkle of 'now I lay me' as she got onto the S-frame; but he heard the scratching.

It came from the communicator and he knew before he went to it what he would find: the record and the thin screeling (the amplifier off as well as the telesender): "I'll kill you!" The call at the Club had been made from his own house.

He stood still for a moment, feeling the enormous bravado of the thing—they must know everything about me! he thought wonderingly—before he remembered to turn the machine off. There was no doubt about it now: they could get.past the doors that were supposed to be sealed to any fingerprint except his own. He felt a kind of terror: could his brother be a part of an organization with such enormous resources? To booby-trap the time-file—to get into an Investigator's own house—that would be difficult enough even for Cary's own technical staff—Instantly he thought of Gannell. The man had his own ways—purely official of course—around most barriers.

Then, for just a moment, he felt something besides his true fear and his anger—exaltation? resignation? He turned the record off.

"Daddio?"

"Coming," he said, still wondering: Gannell? Levin? His brother? X? And tried to think of his wife in a different and more warmblooded way.

He dropped his clothing and got onto the S-frame.

Immediately he was angry. He felt the betraying softness under him and knew that she had turned up the force field to maximum and he resented it. It was his own private heresy—his solitary vice—to sleep on the S-frame (two army cots stretched drumtight and stitched together) without the anti-gravity field. Now, bitterly, he threshed about—or tried to—suspended in the solid, conforming and expensive air, hugging his own side of the field.

"Let's go to bed, Daddio," she said wistfully.

"Dammit, we *are* in bed!"

"What do you mean?"

"What they used to *sleep* in," he said with exaspera-

80

tion. "In the past, they called it a bed."

"So *that's* why we say it," Lulubel said tenderly. "You're so smart. You know what I *mean*, daddio. Punch my ticket."

"All *right!*"

Mechanically, manfully, moderately, unmerrily, he became part of the beast with two backs, did his devoir.

As often happened, he ended by nearly enjoying it.

"Gee, you're not bad, Daddio," Lulubel said professionally. "You always surprise me."

It was flattery, and he knew it, and he was pleased. "Thanks," he said, liking her as he often, to his sometimes surprise, found himself doing.

"Gee, if you only didn't go to business every day, I'll bet you'd be a real stick man."

"Thanks." He only vaguely understood her meaning —a part of the jargon of Amalgamated Joy, he supposed —but he was pleased again. Then curious: "What do you mean about going to business?" he asked.

"I don't know exactly. There's a song we used to sing: 'An engineer loves his slide-rule'—I don't know what it *says* but I know what it *means*, and it means that people who go to business and are engineers and stuff just have a real hard time getting *up* there. Or Beaters. Or Joy Boys like the Mohawks and Hellfire Club that go around beating up people. People like that—Beaters and all—they just don't have it. It's like they used it all up in their work. Or maybe they just like their work better than sex. The mean ones just aren't any good in bed. Except when they're being mean."

"Oh."

81

He had stopped listening to her. What she was saying was a part of her 'mystery,' a part of the folklore of the sodality to. which she had belonged before he married her. He was not interested in the knowledges of Joy Girls. The Investigator lay on his own side of the S-frame and tried to sleep.

"—and so I left," Lulubel was saying. "I didn't want to do *that* all the time. Besides I always *did* want to be a *wife,* sort of. When I was in Amalgamated Joy—"

The Investigator slept.

And dreamed:

——"Stop it," his father said. "Stop it, stop it, stop it, stop it. What's that you've got in your hand?" He looked and it was a small bird. "Nasty thing," his father said and the bird writhed and he could feel snaky coils on his arm. "Don't you know you'll go insane if you do?" his father said. "I'll have to punish you." Whack! Whack! and the good feeling. Smack! "A bellywhopper!" Chris yelled. They were swimming, the bunch of them, but he sat on the bank, for some reason he couldn't go into the water. "Come on," Chris said. "It's good. It makes you feel clean even inside." "I mustn't," he said; "I'll tell on you. You know we're not supposed to. Come out of the water." "I can't," Chris said. "I've got to save somebody." And he felt himself rooted to the bank as he watched his brother's head bob far out on the water. Something was tearing him apart. "Stop it," he told himself. "They're only swimming." Someone was calling for help. He heard his own voice but it was also the voice of Chris far out in the water and he saw the head bobbing toward shore and felt both anger and release.

82

"Aren't you going to punish me?" he asked. "You are not your brother's keeper," his mother said. "He might have drowned." "You are not your brother's keeper." He turned to her, whimpering. "I was supposed to watch. Aren't you going to punish me?" "You didn't go swimming, why should I punish you?" his father said. "Stop it! What's that you've got in your hand?" It was the bird, but it was dead now. There was someone else in the room. He stood in the corner and he had no face. "Aren't you going to punish me?" he asked the faceless man. "My name is Jones," the man said. "I am for justice, not punishment." Sick with shame and rage he tried to shout at them: "I'm here! I'm here!" but no one noticed him, not even his father. "It's your *fault!*" he shouted and flung the dead bird at the faceless man, but it stuck to his hand, and just then the naked girl——

And woke, hearing the bird in his garden sing the serene mechanical and definitive note. He was sweating and trembling. "You son-of-a-bitch, I'll turn you off in the morning, I'll cut off *your* juice!" he silently promised the bird, and turning on his other side disposed himself once more toward the dark country of sleep.

("—and that's why it's different," Lulubel was saying. "Besides when you're a wife, you got *privileges.* Mate. Helpmeet. You got a right to love somebody, you can even help him. Slippers. Have the Psychomat ready. Turn on the garden. In sickness and in health. A hard but honorable estate—'dignified and commodious sacrament' the Matrimonial Engineer said. You know what that means, daddio? 'Signifying matrimonie. Necessarye coniunction.' Conjunction—gee, you *are* good, daddio.

83

'Whiche betokeneth concorde.' In the old days they even had children themselves. Bore them. *That's* a funny word. Why *bore?* Nowadays we don't, but I bet we could. I bet I could. So then I left Amalgamated Joy—")

The Investigator slept.

And dreamed:

——It was a very big city that he was in—he did not know what city it was but he knew that it was big—and he was lost. He seemed to be in a travel machine of some sort, and after a while he came to a house. It was an enormous house. The walls—massive, dark, sullen rock covered with heroic bas-reliefs—flowed up and over the hills like a vast and stony serpent. Then he was in some sort of garden, an odd one with real trees and flowers in it, and there was a great stone terrace going up to the house. There was someone on the terrace and he tried to call, to ask where he was, to ask—but he didn't know what he wanted to ask. Did he want to ask where he was? It seemed foolish, because he had the feeling that he should *know* where he was. He was trying to find someone, that was it. But who was it he wanted? The person on the terrace was a relative, he knew, of the person for whom he was searching. He felt an enormous urgency: Ask! Ask! and he tried to think: whom was he trying to find? Suddenly something happened—the rising of the wind? a cloud over the moon? (he became aware that it was night)—and the aspect of the garden changed: it grew heavy, portentous, thick with evil—someone was watching him. Now he was fixed in horror—he wanted to leave, to run, but the walls went on into the distance; and beyond was only the alien city and he needed to find the one he was looking for. In an agony he tried to force his tongue to utter the name, to call out, and in his terror and his need he began to remember it. It was——

"Yes?"

Stupified with sleep, with the terror and the urgency of the dream still in him, he woke to find himself standing before the communicator. It had wakened him. The soft, whispering bleat of his name had cut through the dream. Or had the dream wakened him first? He *had* been dreaming, he remembered. A nightmare—he could still feel the fear. He shook himself into wakefulness and irritability and switched on the machine. It was Gannell; the square ugly head swam into focus like a coastal promontory emerging out of fog.

"Hello, chief."

"For Christ's sake!" Cary said, "did you have to wake me up at this hour?"

Automatically he looked at his watch: he had slept perhaps fifteen minutes.

"Sorry," Gannell said in a business-like voice. "Big news just came in. They sent it over to me from the office. Got *me* up too."

"All right," Cary said, yawning. "What is it?"

"The Private Eye is coming. The Grand Inquisitor. The Big One Himself."

"Make sense, won't you!" Cary said. "I'm dead for sleep. What are you talking about?"

"I tell you *he's* coming."

"*Who?*"

"Jones. Himself," Gannell said impatiently. "The

Grand Inquisitor. What's the matter—aren't you awake yet?"

"I don't understand. Jones? You mean *the* Jones, the one that we gave all those crazy names to? The one that doesn't even *exist?*"

"Oh, he exists all right," Gannell laughed shortly. "I thought the same thing—that he was just an invention of the Punishment Department, something the L.A.P.D. had made up to keep us all on our toes. But he's real enough to talk to—they just did at the office anyway."

"But *I'm* the Investigator!" Cary said.

"Sure, but so is he. He's the real one, the real *big* one. Unless they have others even bigger that not even the P.D. knows anything about." Gannell paused for a moment as if thinking about it. Something like awe touched his face. "Could be, I suppose," he added. "Ad infinitum —you know—the littler bugs have littler bugs."

Cary was not listening to him. Something back in a corner of his brain was trying to tell him something. He remembered now all the jokes—shoptalk and therefore by definition not seditious—he had heard about the man they nick-named the Grand Inquisitor. But he had never believed him real. A jape by Gannell? He didn't even have to look at the screen to know that Gannell was not joking—was not even capable of such a joke, Cary thought. Then it was true—there was another Investigator, someone higher up than himself? He felt the solid stuff of the world suddenly blown thin as gossamer and himself hanging over the void, sustained only in a vast and trembling web. He groped toward an acceptance and an understanding of the existence of Jones.

"All right," he said finally. "What does he want?" In his mind a procession of Joneses marched, an infinite regress, on all the roads of time. Thinking of them he felt less lonely—since there were other Investigators besides himself. But he felt like nothing, like the littler bug. Could he really believe that Jones existed?

"I don't know what he wants," Gannell said. "A message came through out here from Central Engineering, that's all."

"Damn it, is that enough to wake me up for? Couldn't you have waited to tell me at the office? You know I've got this other thing I'm working on. My brother——" He had intended to tell Gannell about the threat against himself, about the message, but something stopped him.

"Oh *that*," Gannell said. "Forget about it. Mistake somewhere. Your brother's dead."

"*What?*"

"Your machine not working properly? I said he was dead. You don't have a brother anymore. Someone got the dossiers mixed up and his went into the active one, that's all."

"But if he's dead then how——" Again Cary broke off.

"What's the matter?" Gannell's head moved and he peered owlishly out of the screen at Cary. "You look like you've seen a ghost. I thought you'd be glad to get the news. Now you can think about that vacation. No need to come in on Monday if you don't want to. I'll handle Jones for you. Unless he wants to see you personally."

Cary forced his voice to hold steady. He could not

look at Gannell now. "Thanks," he said. "Thanks, Gannell. Mighty good of you."

"I just thought you'd want to have it off your mind, in case you had any sentimental feeling about the case. After all, he *was* your brother. And when they gave me the word about Jones, they told me the case had been closed. Decision of someone higher up—maybe Jones himself. Anyway, I just thought you'd want to know as soon as possible. Sorry about waking you."

"That's all right. Thanks." Now he did look at Gannell, but the graven face of the man told him nothing. No, Gannell could not be joking, but there should be *something* he could read in the face. There was nothing. "Thanks," Cary said again. 'Call you soon." And snapped off the switch.

In the dark of the room with the idiot mechanical birdsong falling around him like a rain of glass beads, Cary tried to focus his thoughts, but at the center of them there was the fear: someone was trying to get him.

There was no other way to interpret the things that had happened: the booby-trapped time-file, the Psychomat which had run amuck, the threat at the Club. Someone was trying to kill him. Chris, his brother.

But then why had Gannell lied to him—why had he said that Chris was dead when Cary himself had evidences of his existence in the attempts that had been made on his life? But Gannell did not know about the attempts— Gannell had assumed that the business with the time-file had been only a malfunction. *Or did he know?* Was he lying so that Cary's brother might have a better chance of succeeding next time, with Cary himself believing his brother dead?

But *why?* Gannell could hardly be in conspiracy with Chris. Or *could* he be? If he *were* a part of a conspiracy, then he must be lying about Chris' death to put Cary off his guard. But perhaps he was telling the truth, in that case——

No. An error of that sort, shifting a case from the dead to the active file—that simply did not, could not happen. The dossiers were too valuable, too well organized and cared for, to allow for an error of that sort.

It followed then that Gannell was *lying.* But why, then, should he have given Cary the file on his brother in the first place? Why not say nothing to Cary, and thereby allow the killer—his brother or whoever it might be—every opportunity to kill the Investigator? Why put the Investigator on the case at all?

Because he had to, Cary decided. Gannell had been given the file and told to have an investigation started on it. Gannell would have been afraid *not* to give it to the Investigator because someone might learn that he had not done so.

But *who* then was responsible for the ridiculous "error" of changing Chris's dossier from the dead to the active file? And *why?* And why *now* had someone ordered Gannell to tell Cary to drop the case *when he knew his brother was alive? Why? Who?*

Suddenly, and for the first time, Cary believed fully in the Grand Inquisitor. A coldness grew all through him —he could see it now: he was being investigated. Whether Gannell was a conspirator or not, Cary saw now that the

89

business with the dossier had been simply a test of himself, to see how he would act. It was a different part of the pattern of events, something apart from Gannell whether or not Gannell was a conspirator, something apart from his brother whether alive or dead. He was being investigated! He felt he wanted to laugh, but his fear did not go away and he was afraid to laugh because he might not be able to stop.

He looked out at the garden into which the early dawn, as grey as pus, was seeping. The bird sang down its clear and imitable note. Everything seemed as solid and real as before, but Cary had a feeling as if he were seeing it for the first time, as if the gross and viable pushiness of the world he had known had given way before some terrible transformation. He did not know where he was —he felt like a shipwrecked seaman drifting in unknown latitudes. He wanted to shout Help! but he knew that no one would be listening.

He pushed back his fear and thought through it again. Crazy as it was, he was probably being investigated, hunted. But he himself was the hunter, the Investigator —whether or not Jones was real, he was still the Investigator. There was a plot of some kind. He would find out about it no matter who was involved: his brother, Gannell—Jones, even, if there was a Jones. There was nothing more to be thought about it now.

(From the bedroom he heard a drowsy giggle. "Don't, daddio. Don't. Don't." Lulubel's voice was coy with sleep.)

For just a moment he wanted to throw it all overboard —his job, his duty, everything. An enormous weariness crushed him. It would be easy to let them—his brother, Gannell, "Jones," whoever it was—get away with their plot—whatever it was. It would be an end to his endless hunt. For just a moment he wanted to end it. To tell Lulubel about it. To cut and run.

But run where?

To confess and be punished and be at peace.

(Again the giggle from the bedroom. "Oh yes, daddio." And a long sigh.)

But he was not guilty of anything.

For a moment he thought with envy of the man he had juiced that afternoon, now turned into a kind of zombie, his memory and will burned out of him, and of the words of the crazy preacher in the park: *He is coming!—The Accuser who is God of this world!* In mortal anguish Cary wished to be a brother of those common and guilty men.

But could not. He was innocent and he was alone.

Wearily he got himself a sleeping pill and wearily he climbed onto the sleeping frame. Lulubel was still talking herself to sleep. He pushed all thought out of his mind and let himself drift toward the dark and promising shore. Then he was aware that she was talking to him.

"Could we, daddio?"

"What?" he asked, trying not to be angry, afraid he would fully awaken.

"Could we? Have a baby of our own?"

All the anger and frustration of the day flushed through him.

"Well for God's sake!" he said savagely. "Can't you

leave me alone? If you want one, for Christ's sake go out and *buy* it!"

For a long time, fighting toward sleep like a swimmer toward a far island, he heard her crying.

Finally the Investigator slept.

And dreamed no more.

III.

And now the Investigator rode in a black tunnel
longer than sleep.

Now, with on both sides of him a shimmer of walls
like vitreous glass, and over him a windy turbulence and
wrack of cloud, and in front of him, precise as logic, the
dead-straight line of the dun-colored highway, the Investigator charged at full speed into the purlieu of the
dream. A feeling of obscure dread filled him: there was
nothing to be seen but the blur of dark at the sides, the
crazy rags of black cloud above him, the hypnotic line of
the road—perhaps he was standing still while the road
spooled under him? He felt that he was driving at break-
neck speed to nowhere at all and pushed the thought
away, telling himself *dust storm* and trying to locate
where he was. It was all filed away there somewhere—
black of the San Joaquin's ruined fields, reddish for the
sand and sandstone of Angelus Crest, the colors of Earth.

The city, when he arrived, seemed empty of everything but echoes. An umber smog burned his eyes and he
slipped his mask on, crossing the square like a soldier ad-
vancing through a gas attack. There was no one around.
Somewhere in the distance he could hear voices, muted in
the heavy smother, and from somewhere else the pad of
feet like an echo of his own. Far as Roncevaux, a horn

sounded; he heard the tired and mocking echo drift across the park and thought, irrelevantly, *Gabriel* and blundered out of the fog against a building.

It should have been his own office building, but it wasn't. There was no door where there should have been one and for a moment he felt again an upsetness, as if reality had shifted, a silent earthquake of number and identity, and it came to him that, ridiculous as it might be, he was lost.

He went on along the wall of the building—it seemed as long as the wall of the nightmare. Then it seemed to him that it must be the building of Amalgamated Joy, and he struck out in what he thought was the direction to his own office building. In a moment he was back against the same wall, as if it had turned with him in the fog; and now, completely disoriented, he began to retrace his steps to the square. Then, surprisingly, in a few steps he was at his own building, but somehow he had got to the back door. There was no identifier plate, and for a moment he thought he would not be able to enter—the door did not know him. Then he found his key and went in.

Now he had to be careful. The office would normally be empty at such an hour, but there might be people in the halls and he did not want to be seen. His feet had begun automatically to walk him to his own office. Then he stopped—what was it he had come for? Then he remembered what he had to do.

The room with the dossiers was downstairs at the end of the hall. He paused on the landing and waited. No sound. He went on quickly and silently down the hall

94

and put his thumb against the identifier plate.

Once he was inside, where the walls were filing cases like the compartments in an old-fashioned morgue, he paused again uncertainly. His mind was as full of fog as the empty city, he thought; and he began once more to feel his way through his anxieties and irrelevancies.

There was a plot against him as proven by the attempts to kill him. An attempt at killing an Investigator was the highest form of sedition. Gannell and Jones—if there was a Jones—must be in on it since they—or at least Gannell—had lied about his brother being dead. His duty as an Investigator was to expose the plot and bring the plotters to punishment.

It was simple enough when he looked at it that way, but somewhere in the last couple of days his feelings had pulled loose from the matrix of his thinking, and he felt an obscure dread as he crossed to the files at the other side of the room. What he was doing now, although he was acting on his own and single authority, was not wrong —there had been more of a flavor of sedition in his purchase of the flowers two days before—but he felt a heaviness and unease, like the residual fear from a forgotten dream. He pulled open the file.

It was there just as he had known it had to be—the file on his brother. Quickly he glanced through it. Yes, it was exactly like the material he had seen the other day. Gannell *had* lied then, and the file itself was proof.

It was when he was putting it back that he noticed the other paper. Somehow it had dropped between the folders and he had missed it. It was a closure form with nothing on it but the suspect's name: Chris Cary, and the two

95

options: PUNISHED and DEAD. The space after DEAD had been checked with a red pencil.

Cary held the form in his hand, unable to believe it. Somewhere out of the past he heard his mother sadly chide him, and himself saying in his whiny boy's voice: Do I always have to take care of *him?* He would never have to look after his brother now, never stand frozen on the bank while his brother was in danger of drowning in the dark pool at the river. Cary felt loss now, as if he were suddenly older. And a cruel joy at the death. And betrayal: he would never, now, show his brother that he had not hesitated out of fear that time at the riverbank.

Then the enormity of the meaning on the slip of paper came to him.

If his brother were dead, then what of the attacks that had been made against himself? For a moment he doubted his own sanity, doubted that the attacks had taken place at all. *Accidents,* his mind said, groping for understanding; *imagination,* said something deeper, a voice out of the dark, a boogieman voice.

Slowly the world settled and came to rest. No, neither accident nor imagination—there could be no doubt at all about the message he had got at the Club, the message he had found on the record in his communicator when he got home. But would Gannell have the nerve to close the file on his brother without official sanction? No; his brother *must* be dead, had probably been dead all the time —but the voice had been so like his brother's!—and Gannell had merely tossed the file to him as a red herring to cover up his own attempts on the life of the Investiga-

96

tor. But did Gannell have that kind of cunning and courage?

It was an unsatisfactory explanation. There was something more he knew—there had to be—and now in the dead air of the room he seemed to feel the presence of something else, the presence, perhaps of someone bigger than Gannell—Jones. He felt stupid, like a man caught in a crazy labyrinth, and had the complicated man's hunger for simplicity and certainty.

There was, of course, the Sibyl.

If he could get to her.

He had done, rather absent-mindedly, a considerable favor for Adam Virgil, the man who had charge of her, and regarded him as a friend. "As much as I have friends," he thought bitterly. Feeling Jones' presence and hearing the ghostly baying of the far and legendary hounds, he told himself in a fury of belief *I'm not guilty.* Had any of the Suspects he had juiced felt this way? The thought shocked him. *You're innocent,* he told himself primly. There was no kinship to be claimed or admitted.

The Sibyl, then. But first he wanted to look at his own file. He pulled open the drawer.

Looking at the file he felt curiously removed, as if he were a spectator at his own laying out. What a lot of stuff they had gathered together about him! But none of it was bad—it was just the routine data he might have expected. There was a question about Lulubel, nothing specific, but it shocked him. "I don't seem to understand anybody," he thought, but it was more fatigue than despair. He took out his dossier and put it in his brief case and closed the door. It was like giving himself up for

97

burial. He went out of the file room and down the long flight of stairs to the place where they kept the giant mechanical brain they called the Sibyl.

As usual, Virgil was somewhere inside, tinkering with the machine. Cary called to him and he came head first out of a manhole in the Sibyl's side, a tiny wrinkled old embryo of a man with a face like a wizened apple.

"Hello," he said. "What brings you here?"

"Hello, Adam. Got some questions for Sibby, if I can use the old girl," Cary said, controlling his eagerness. "Any objections?"

"I don't know," Virgil said doubtfully. "You got a permit?"

"No. This isn't anything special. I didn't know I'd need one."

"I suppose it's all right," Adam Virgil said. He crossed the room to his desk, rummaged in a drawer for some waste, and wiped his hands. "I just take care of her. I don't care what she's used for."

"Good," Cary said. "And thanks. It's a real favor."

"Wait till you've talked to her before you thank me," Virgil said. "People don't always like what she tells them."

"I'll take a chance."

"Yes," Virgil said. "They all do." He finished washing his hands and sat down at his desk. "She doesn't seem to be working so well," he said.

"What's the matter with her?"

"Don't know. Nothing I can find out. Some say she's

sick—neurotic. That's the head-shrinkers for you—they got an explanation for everything." He shoved the waste back in the drawer, took out a lunch-box and noisily snapped it open. "Apple?" he asked, holding one out toward the Investigator.

Automatically Cary took it. "How does she behave?" he asked.

"Gives funny answers—that's what *they* say. But my notion is, ask a silly question you get a silly answer. Anyway, that's how she got her name—giving odd answers sometimes." Virgil stuck half a sandwich into his shriveled mouth and began to chew slowly.

"What do you mean?"

"Sybil," Virgil said. "It means something like someone who sometimes asks a riddle. Somebody named her that a couple of centuries ago, I guess. Now ask me why this place is called the Cave."

"Is it?"

"Sure. Only nobody knows that but me. My father told me that. He used to take care of her before he died and I inherited his job. I guess somebody told him it was called that."

"Well," Cary said. "What seems to be wrong with her?"

"If you want my opinion," Virgil said, chewing, "nothing's wrong with her. It's something wrong with them."

"What do you mean?"

"Maybe they ask her questions that can't be answered. Or something stupid. So maybe she makes a joke."

"I shouldn't think she'd do that——" Cary began.

99

"Look," Virgil gestured at the Sybil squatting massively at the far end of the enormous room. "Here she is. She's got more brains than any ten or ten thousand men ever dreamed of having between them. Suppose you was her and some stupid character come along and wakes you up just to ask some stupid question. Don't you think you might make a joke about it?"

"Well," Cary said doubtfully. "I——"

"Suppose somebody comes and asks you: 'How can I live forever?' What do you tell him? Or somebody who is worthless comes and asks you: 'How good a man am I?' Do you think you could give either of them a satisfactory answer? So when the generals come and ask the Sybil: 'How long will the Pretend War last?' don't you think she's got a right to her little joke?"

"What did she say?"

"She said 'How long do you want it to last?'" Virgil said. "And they didn't like *that* much. The thing is, people don't *want* a real answer any more. They want to be assured that they already *know* what's right. And the Sybil knows that, and she don't want to reassure anybody. So she makes her jokes."

"Well," Cary said. "I don't have impossible questions to ask her. Or stupid ones."

"Sure not," Virgil said. "Nobody does." He crumpled the wrapping of the sandwich and dropped it into the waste basket. "You want to cut a tape, or talk to her?"

"Talk, I guess. It'd be hard to formulate the questions."

"All right," Virgil said indifferently. "I'll get out for a while. I don't want to be knowing any of *your* business." He snapped the lunch-box closed and went out of the room.

With Virgil gone, Cary felt an odd uneasiness, as if he were in the presence of a living being. All around him, along the walls, were the enclosed banks of the Sybil's circuits. At the other end of the room, on a kind of dais, was the squarish shape of the answering device: a dome-shaped cloudy head from which ticker-tape dangled like pale hair, and below this "head," in the "torso," the small dark orifice of the speaker. From where Cary stood, the Sibyl looked like some grotesque Buddha of heroic proportions dreaming on a divan, her great milky head, as if made of cloud, inclined slightly, favoring her navel with a benign and unregardant stare.

He went forward and seated himself at the small control table in front of the figure.

"Greetings," she said in a tired voice.

Cary had the momentary feeling that someone had played a practical joke on him. Then he thought: *The switch is in the chair seat.* And leaned across the table and said "Hello," awkwardly, like an actor in an amateur performance.

"You have not brought the portion for the god," the Sibyl told him in her dusty voice.

"What?"

"The requisition. You're supposed to place it in the time-clock and have it punched."

"Oh." Frantically Cary rummaged in his pockets until he found a slip of paper. He pushed the end of it into the slot of the desk and there was a crickety sound and the chime of a bell, as if from the timer for a three-minute egg.

"Thank you," said the Sibyl. "It is not the golden bough, but then we are a long way from Avernus. And in any case you have slaughtered your four bullocks, have you not?"

"Yes," Cary said, sweating, thinking: *she's crazy as a loon;* and sat up straight in the chair and said: "I have a question to ask."

"Ask it."

Now that he was there, with the solution only a second away, Cary found himself tongue-tied. His mind, full of questions, flickered like a Fourth of July sparkler, but he did not know what to ask.

"Put your thinking cap on," the Sibyl told him, and her dry voice, like a rasping of dead leaves, seemed to have a terrible patience in it. Patience or indifference.

"It's right there beside you," she said, and Cary saw the little metallic cap with its antennae of wires on a stand beside the desk. "Put it on and I can read you. It will save much of the talk."

Cary put the little metal skull-cap on his head and tried to arrange his thoughts. He tried to start out very simply, in the way that he had reasoned when he had looked at his brother's file. He started over it, just as he had reasoned it out before. If his brother were dead. . . .

"You are looking for Palinurus," the Sibyl said. "But he is drowned."

"But he didn't drown." Cary said quickly, seeing again in his mind the dark river, the bobbing head, his own weakness and hesitation.

102

"You mean your brother. Yes. Long has he pulled at the oar.

"Is he alive?" Cary asked. It was one of the questions he had been frantic to ask.

For a long time the Sibyl said nothing. Then there was something like a rusty sigh.

"He is as alive as you," she said.

"Good," he said exultantly. "Then Gannell falsified the file on him. Is Gannell guilty?"

"Yes."

Now I have them, Cary thought with a fierce joy. *Now——*

"As guilty as anyone," the Sibyl said indifferently.

Cary felt as if he had been slapped in the face. "What do you mean?" he asked.

For a long time there was nothing but a humming silence, like the sound of his own blood in his ears. Had the Sibyl really said anything at all, he wondered, afraid that he might have imagined it. It was like the dream of last night——

The Sibyl began speaking:

Two gates the silent house of Sleep adorn:
Of polished ivory this, that of transparent horn;
True visions through transparent horn arise;
Through polished ivory pass deluding lies.

Cary listened to her with a growing sense of unreality, of being trapped in a nightmare. When she had finished there was a pause and again the dry humming sound, sunny as bees. He did not know what to say.

"That," the Sibyl said, "is by Virgil. With some help from a man named Dryden."

"Listen," Cary said in desperation. "Jones. Is he real?"

After a moment the Sibyl said: "I got the impression *your* name was Jones."

"It's an official name, a name we use in our work," Cary said impatiently. "And all Stool-pigeons use it. But this particular Jones, is he real?"

"As real as you. As real as any Jones."

Cary was sick with the confirmation of his greatest fear; sick, too, of the guarded or riddling answers he had received. The thought of having the solution to the mystery of what was happening to him in his grasp, yet not to be able to understand it, make him frantic. In a great effort of concentration, like a man lifting a super-human weight, he pulled all his thoughts together and tried to formulate one question that he had to have answered.

"Who is guilty?" he asked in a strangled voice. "Who is guilty?"

Again the pause, the sunny and bee-like buzzing: a classical sound, pure as spring water.

"Everyone," the Sibyl said. "Everyone in his own degree."

"But who? *Who?*"

"That is for man to answer," the Sibyl said. "I am only a machine."

Clumsily, crazily, carefully, the Investigator took off the little skull-cap and placed it on its stand. He felt drunk with disappointment and despair. He got up and turned to the door.

"——something he carries on his back," the Sibyl said. "Which I am forbidden to see."

He was almost at the door.

"You have forgotten something."

"What do you want?" Cary asked, recording automatically that the switch had not been in the chair seat after all.

"I want to die," the Sibyl said, as if very weary. "But you have forgotten something. Punch your ticket?"

Cary came slowly back to the desk and held the end of the paper in the jaws of the time-clock. Crickets. *Br-r-ring.* He went toward the door.

"I can only give you the wisdom and help of the past," the Sibyl told him. "The past cannot answer your questions as you want them answered. Datta. Dayadhvam. Damyata."

B-z-z-z. Click. Fragments of the past.

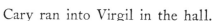

Cary ran into Virgil in the hall.

"Go all right?" Virgil asked.

"Oh—yes, all right," Cary said with effort. He pulled his face into a smile like a grimace. "Thanks again. I won't forget you." Turning toward the elevators.

"Elevators not working," Virgil said. "Long way up to the light, too."

"Yes."

"Gets lonesome stuck away down here, nobody to talk to but the Sibyl."

"Interesting company," Cary said. He started up the stairs. At the landing he remembered something and turned. "I didn't know you wrote poetry," he said. "Not bad either." He tried to sound judicious.

Climbing the second stair.

———o———

Now he was once more in the fog.

Coming outside the building it was thick and there was an acid sting in it stronger than before. He clapped his mask on and walked around the corner and came face to face with Gannell.

He recognized the square-built figure immediately in spite of the mask the other man was wearing, and he stood stock still. Gannell halted before walking into him and there began a crazy kind of gavotte, like the dance of mating birds, as Gannell tried to pass him. Then Cary stood still again and the other man, muttering an apology or a curse (through the mask it was impossible to tell which) went around him.

Didn't recognize me, Cary thought in high wonder. And again he had the awful feeling of alienation he had felt when he had removed his file from the case. *Didn't know me.* And lucky for you, his mind told him, rationally enough. But all he could feel was the sense of non-existence, an anguish of the soul, as if he had become a ghost, but a ghost in a rational house where no one was willing to see him.

106

He went on across the square. It was nearly empty. Here and there he heard a workless stiff moving in the bushes, and there was one small fire, but the comfortable and homely smell of coffee which had filled the park the night before was no longer present. The flowers were all shut up and the fountain lake was withered, and no bird sang.

Then through the woolly air he heard the sound of the crazy Preacher. He went on across the park toward the sound of the voice.

He was preaching to the mountain. Where before there had been a ring of men, now the old man had only the November-colored and untenanted air for his audience.

"——and only indifference and solidarity can save you," the Preacher was saying. "*Now hear this,* for the time is approaching, the hour of the Accuser. Out of the past and the dark counties of the human heart, and into our gilded and only present, he approaches to lay his stony hand on the quick flower of our wish. There is no escaping him, go as you will to the east or south, take shelter in the barrens of the black north, he will find you out.

"For go where you wish, do you not leave an invisible trail, the spoor of your striving and unrepentant will? Whom have you forgiven? To whom have you prayed in the dark nights? Only to the God of your flesh, or to luck, or to the flesh of another. And what has been your long holiday from hell but a rage of flesh, a cold lust of the mind, the hungry demons of the insatiable will?

"Still, there is time, before the hour of the destroyer, the hour when the ego itself distills a poison, when all

107

your nets catch only your running and crazy self, the time of unmasking and of recognitions. Yes, there is time still if you will use it, time to repent and surrender, the time of admission of guilt. There is still time for punishment, or time for salvation.

"For salvation is offered, and it is born out of the death of the will. Let yourselves fall asleep for a moment—there is time, for it is always the midnight and black deep of love: sleep in that cloud of unbeing.

"For that love is not a hunger for any thing, but the pure hunger itself; it is not a giving of any thing, but the pureness of giving—not an auction of those poor moveables of your whoreson stinking and tagalong body, but a Christmas and a Boxing Day when the piñata of the spirit is broken and goodness showers out common as rain or sin.

"Then you may be born to the new dispensation, beyond the hunger of the flesh and the burning and unresting will, into a solidarity toward your fellow man, a solidarity toward all the living and unliving world, and into an indifference that is first of all an indifference to the self. That is the true coin of the human realm—indifference on one side, a solidarity on the other. That is God's money, who has never lost a toss."

The old man stopped speaking. Then, after a short pause, he said "I thank all of you for listening." There was no one listening except the Investigator. The Preacher got down from the bench.

"Thank you for listening, Mr. Investigator," he said.

"How did you know it was I?" Cary asked in surprise. He was still wearing his mask.

"Oh, it's not hard," the old man said. "You just have to have a gift for it. I'd recognize you anywhere."

"Why do you preach if no one is listening?"

"Why, it's my calling. Don't you investigate even if there is no one to investigate? It's your nature, isn't it?"

Cary did not feel like refuting the nonsense. "Do you believe what you preach?"

The Preacher did not appear surprised at the question. "Yes, I believe it," he said. "The day of the Accuser is coming. You must know it too."

"And you believe that what you've been preaching is the way to get to heaven?"

"Oh, heaven," the Preacher said, shrugging his shoulders. "That's something else again. I'm not interested in heaven. I'm interested in now. I'm interested in the *present*, aren't you?"

"I'm interested in all of the time," Cary said, feeling that in some subtle way he was losing a stupid argument —if it was an argument.

"That's what it is," the Preacher said. "The present *is* all of time—all you can ever really experience. That's why it's most important. That is the wisdom of the present."

"All right," Cary said. The crazy conversation had cheered him up a bit and he had forgotten his own problems for the moment. "Will you give me your blessing?"

"What for? My blessing is no good to you. It's your own blessing you need. Excuse me now. I must preach again." He got up on the bench once more. "Behold," he said in his loud preaching voice. "The Accuser has come, he is here among you, and is clothed in the body of a man!"

Cary went on across the park toward the car creche. At the corner, light flashed—an aureole, the nimbus of a crazy saint. Hunched, laboring, heavy with the weight of this world and the next, the Hand lubberly navigated the blond sea of fog, his light brightening the corner where he was.

"Hello," Cary said. It was the Hand he had spoken to the day before. But there was no obsequiousness in the Hand now.

"Fuck off, Jack," the Hand said thickly. He described an eccentric circle and came to rest facing Cary from the opposite direction. "'Nves'gator," he said, scornfully and again Cary felt the shock of being recognized.

"I saw you last night," he said.

"Thass't *you* think," the Hand said belligerently. "How'd you know it wasn't my brother? How'd you know it wasn't me just *looking* like me? Damn 'Vesa-gator!" He did a tight turn to Cary's left. "Lef's fer bad luck," the Hand confided, coming to rest against the Investigator's right shoulder. "*You* didn't know it'uz me," he said slyly. "*I* recanized *you*. C'mon now, tella truth . . . 'f you c'd recanize a difference in people, howja keep yer job? So ya *din't* recanize me, see?" He gave Cary's shoulder a comradely and alcoholic pat which nearly landed the Investigator in the gutter. "Listen," the Hand said. "Fer *that* part of it, I c'd fergive ya 'f the others could."

"What do you mean?" Cary asked. *Call the Beaters*, his head told him; but he was too tired: the weight of all

110

humanity leaned on his right shoulder. "If who could forgive me?"

"*Famly!*" the Hand said. "Who ya think? Got the biggest fuckin family in the fuckin world. Ya mean ya never heard of us?" He leered. "Listen, pal, if a tree falls in the forest an' yer not around, does it make a noise?"

He leaned on Cary's shoulder, breathing the fumes of alcohol and philosophy: the Investigator remembered uncomfortably his talk with Levin the night before. "Th' Ide family," the Hand said confidentially. "Bigges' ina world. Mean ya don't know my brother Vance T. 'r Mark, 'r Angelo? Buddy-O, you just ain't been *there*." He shifted his weight and the spellcast blazed. "'N sisters till hell won't have it, 'n then all them goddam in-laws to boot. *Both* here 'n in the Unoccupied Country. Lissen, buddy-boy, you know we got more land out there than you guys got here? 'N someday . . . someday. . . ."

"Someday what?" Cary asked, trying to shift the cross that had been granted him.

"*Pf-f-f-ft,* thass all. Jus' *pf-f-f-ft,*" the Hand said darkly.

"Fine," said Cary, trying to break himself loose.

"Gonna be *different,*" the Hand said. "*All* different. I donno how, but I'll see *everything's* different, even things I *like*."

"Excellent," Cary said. He was now actively engaged in trying to get loose from the man.

" 'N you don't believe it," the Hand said bitterly. "You think us Ide's just scum 'n all you gotta do is keep us in

111

our place. *Spellcasts!*—you think thass enough? I'm a builder, 'n I'm gonna take back the machines. You think I'm drunk? I'm drunk on the *future*, thass how I'm drunk! Lissen," he said, heavily confidential. "Tell ya something. It's the future that counts, see?"

"Yes," Cary said, and the thought of Gannell, of Jones, stabbed at him. "It's the future that counts."

"Now ya *got* it," the Hand said happily. He pulled loose from Cary and tried to walk. He couldn't. "Carry me along to the next station, buddy?" he asked. "I c'n make it from there."

"Carry yourself along," the Investigator said. He was suddenly tired with the man's drunken nonsense and ashamed of himself for not calling the Beaters. "Your future is in front of you," he said. "Walk right into it."

"Well, fuck you, Jack," the Hand said. He straightened up and gave Cary a solid, hating look. "Ya had yer chance," he said mysteriously and walked away, going in the plumb-straight line of a man afraid of the slightest deviation. Or had he really been drunk? Cary wondered.

At the corner he turned and went out of sight. "The future doesn't extend very far," Cary thought wryly, but he couldn't make a joke out of it; the thought of his own future filled him with a sick dread.

And went on to the car-creche.

And was borne, in his time, through the cloud of his anxieties and suspicions, out of the black tunnel of the dust-storm, to the locked door of his by now evening-shadowed home.

"Well," Lulubel said, her voice showing her relief,

112

"I'm glad you're back. I thought you'd gone out walking in your sleep again."

"I feel like it," Cary said.

"What is it, honey? What's the matter?"

"Does something have to be the matter?"

"You don't run off like this on a Sunday morning and be gone all day for nothing."

"No.. Not for nothing."

"Can't you tell me?"

A part of him, nauseated with his anxieties and his secrets, wanted to speak. He felt the dead weight of the problem crushing him; he wanted to shift the weight. He looked at his wife: pretty, blonde, powdered and painted and curled, and looked past the worry at the glitter of the joy-girl, and then looked through her without seeing her at all, and said: "There's nothing to tell," and went on into his study and put away the file and rigged the trap for whoever would come.

And came back into the living room again.

"I'm going over to see Levin," he said. Because he had to talk to someone.

Levin was reading. He put the reading spool away and apologized. "Sunday's always a bore to me," he said. "You want a drink?"

"I've got to talk to you."

"Better have a drink anyway," Levin said.

"I've got a problem," the Investigator said. "I——"

"Just a minute," Levin said. He jumped to his feet and went out of the room. Cary could hear the clink of a bottle against a glass. Then something else; the click of a switch—Levin was putting the conversation on tape.

For a moment Cary was shaken with pure outrage; then he felt a cold humor in the circumstance. *Protecting himself,* he thought; and for just a moment he knew an abysmal and shocking self-pity, as if he had said aloud "Nobody loves me." He could feel the blush on his cheek. He took the drink that Levin extended to him.

"This is my problem," Cary said, and told it all as coldly and objectively as he could. "That's it," he said, when he was finished. "What do you think of it?"

While Cary had told the story Levin had been fidgeting in his chair. Now he got up and poured himself another drink, slopping it in the glass, and downed it in a gulp.

"God damn it," he said, "why did you have to pick on me? Why tell me about your problems? I've got problems of my own."

"Wanted to get another point of view," Cary said. It was as close as he could get to asking for help.

"But, damn it, *why me?*"

"I thought you were my friend."

"Friend! A man in your job doesn't have any friends!"

"All right," Cary said. He got up and went to the door.

"You didn't learn anything from the Sibyl?"

"Just what I told you."

"Why should they be after you?"

"I don't know. There's a conspiracy or an investigation. Maybe both. But it's the investigation I can't understand. *Why?* It scares me. I've tried to think. Believe me I've *wanted* to remember something I was guilty of. Can you imagine what it's like to know that they're

114

after you *and not know what for?* It's enough to make you think you're going crazy."

"I suppose so," Levin said. He shrugged his shoulders in defeat. "Sit down," he said. "There isn't anything I can say to help you, but you might as well sit down. I can't throw you out at a time like this."

He got up and went out of the room and again Cary heard the click of a switch. "Might as well tell you I taped all that," Levin said as he came back into the room. He gave a little laugh. "I wiped it off. It's a hell of a note when neighbors can't talk with each other without taking precautions."

"I suppose so," Cary said. He sat down.

"I never though I'd feel sorry for you," Levin said. "But I do now. You've got your hand caught in the machine, and it's a machine you helped build and you know it won't let go. In a sense it doesn't matter what you've done, or if you've done anything——"

"But that's not just!"

"If they take you in and juice you, won't 'justice' be done? Official justice? How many people do you think have been juiced simply on suspicion?"

Cary thought of the man the day before. *If not guilty now, then next week*—that was what he had thought concerning the man.

"But this is *me!*" the Investigator said.

"Don't you think all the men you've juiced have said that?" Levin asked quietly. "Look, I'm going to tell you something. It won't do you any good, but I'm going to tell it to you anyway. It's this: Man wants to be free. He may not know exactly what he means by being free,

115

but that's what he wants. You and your kind have turned society into a man-trapping machine, a real paranoid circus. There's only one end for something like that: after you get all the seditioners, you'll start trapping yourselves. That's what's happened to you—unless you're imagining the whole thing. You haven't any real proof of a conspiracy against you anyway, have you?"

"It's real enough," Cary said. A moment earlier he had felt a sense of release, as if Levin were telling him something true and important; now he felt let down— the man had nothing to offer but platitudes.

Levin seemed to sense the withdrawal. He got up. "Got to go down and work on a spellcast," he said. "Last one. I'm quiting the racket. No. don't leave," he told the Investigator who had been on the point of rising. "Finish your drink. Claire'll be in in a minute." He paused at the door and turned back. "Give you some good advice," he said. "Quit. Go on a long vacation— maybe this whole thing'll blow over."

"It *won't* blow over!"

"Then there's nothing to do but run," Levin said. He was cool now, as if he regretted having spoken frankly a moment before. "Sometimes there aren't any easy answers." He stood at the door as if thinking of something. "Look," he said finally, "you know there's a big opposition to your crazy system. This could finish me, but if you want to run for it, I'll help you get out to the Unoccupied Country."

Cary knew the risk Levin was offering to take, and knew that it was offered not even out of friendship or even pity, but only from some kind of solidarity or abstract notion of justice; and he felt a consuming hatred for the other man.

"God damn you," he said. "You forget whom you're talking to. I could get you juiced for saying a thing like that. And I'm *innocent*, you bastard, innocent!"

"Suit yourself," Levin said and went out, and a moment later Cary heard the rasp of the door of the car stall.

"Daddio!"

Clarabel crossed the room toward him going a bit unsteadily, a little drunk. "Gee, I'm glad you're here. You know it get's lonesome all by yourself?"

"I was just leaving," Cary said stiffly and got up.

"What's the matter?" She gave him a quick trying-to-be-sober look. She put her arms around his neck and cocked her head coquettishly. "You got troubles?"

"We've all got troubles," he said, trying to disentangle himself, to set down his drink, moving with her arms pinioning him, like a man in a sack race.

"Me too," Clarabel said. "I'm sorry you got troubles, Johnny. I got troubles too, Johnny. Maybe we should put our troubles together. I got just the thing for your troubles."

"It will pass," Cary said, trying harder now to free himself and feeling every movement he made complemented and answered with an assured and astonishing and quite reckless lubricity by Clarabel. In a crazy farce of rape he found himself being danced heavily and obscenely into the sleeping room, felt the sleeping frame against his legs before he toppled onto it, thought of Jones and the hunt that was up for him, and said in wonder and outrage out of a cloud of perfumed flesh: "This has got to stop!"

"Got just the thing for trouble, Daddio," Clarabel crooned.

He wrenched himself loose. "Damn it!" he said in flaming anger. "Don't you think of anything else?"

"What else is there?"

He felt the weight of her breasts; her face came down on his, spreading out as his eyes went out of focus, as big as the moon. He slapped her as hard as he could.

"You bitch!" he said, struggling up from the sleeping frame.

"Are you angry?" Holding her hand to her cheek, she looked like a child that had been punished.

"You whore!"

She looked at him as if wondering if it were a joke. He straightened his clothes and wiped the lipstick from his face.

"You rotten tramp! You've never wanted anything else in your life, have you?"

Clarabel sat up on the sleeping frame. "*I* wanted!" she said contemptuously. "I was trying to *give* you something, you son-of-a-bitch!"

"You damned women think anything can be fixed by going to bed! Thanks for the offer!"

"You bastards haven't left us anything else to give!"

She got up and went past him into the living room and picked up a drink.

"I always liked you, Johnny. Everybody thought you were a cold fish and hated you or were afraid of you, but I liked you. And I *do* want to help you if you're in trouble—I mean I *did* want to. But nobody can help you.

118

You won't let anyone help you. You're a monster, a cold, crazy monster and I'm sick of you. Now get out!"

She left the room, and the Investigator, his clothing in order once more, and his face impassive, and his mind full of furies and disasters, went out the door and across the garden and into his house.

———o———

Lulubel was waiting for him in the living room. He started past her toward his study but she stopped him.

"Johnny, you've got to tell me what's the matter. We've got to talk."

"There's nothing to talk about."

"You can say that when I've never seen you so upset before! What *is* it, Johnny? I've got a right to know."

"Just some business." He was beyond caring now, he did not want to talk to anyone, it had been a mistake to ask anyone for help. "Not your business, anyway."

"But it is my business, Johnny. That's what a wife is for, isn't it? To help the man she loves?"

"Oh, yes," he said, and laughed shortly, full of despair. "Love. I thought we'd get around to love pretty soon."

"It's what a wife's for, Johnny," she said quietly. "I want to help you. I'll do anything."

"Will you shut up then?" he asked savagely. "Will you let me alone? What could you do—take me out to the club? take me to bed with you?"

"Johnny, if you're in trouble I'll do anything. If it's something bad why don't we go away? We could run away to the Unoccupied Country and——"

"Wouldn't that be nice," he sneered. "Lulubel the joy-girl pioneer. Who'd do your nails for you then?"

"You can laugh if you want to, but I'd go with you. I wouldn't care how hard it was. Do you think all I care about is this?" She swept her hand in a gesture at the room, the house, her life. "Do you think I *like* this? Don't you think I'm sick of being a—a concubine? Don't think *I'd* be giving up so much!"

What she had said astonished him. He was not used to having her think.

"Well, nobody's going anywhere," he said shortly.

"What *is* the trouble, Johnny."

"Gannell. Jones. I don't know who. There's a conspiracy against me. They're after me."

"Oh, Johnny!" He could see her terror plainly now, and it pleased him. "Then we'll have to go. It's your only chance."

"I'm not going. I'm not going to let them do this to me. I'm innocent. I'm *not* going, and that's flat."

"No," Lulubel said and he could hear the defeat in her voice. "No, you're not going, and that finishes us. Innocent! Do you know what it means to be innocent, Johnny? Do you feel innocent?"

"Of course I do."

"Well, I don't."

"You don't?" He looked at her in puzzlement and surprise, as if she were a stranger. "Why?"

"Because I'm *not*. Don't you think I know about the men you've juiced, about all the so-called conspirators you've hunted? And why did you hunt them? To keep us and people like us in these fine houses in the suburbs. To subsidize Amalgamated Joy. To pay for Club Night.

120

To keep you in your job so you could hunt down other men so that a handful of us could enjoy Wholly Using, Wholly Living. And what about the Hands, the Workless Stiffs? And when you come right down to it, what about people like me or like Clarabel, leading a useless existence, just to be handy when you want us? I thought I was lucky, because I loved you, but what about the others who *don't* love their husbands? And you ask me why I don't feel innocent!"

"You're hysterical," he said stiffly. "I've done nothing but my duty."

"Yes," she said, and got to her feet slowly, as if bone-tired. "That ends it then. There's nothing left to do but say goodbye. You haven't got any real use for me, Johnny. You won't let me help you. You won't quit, get out, go away. Can you really say that you want me to stay with you?"

She waited for him to speak and when he said nothing she turned to the door.

"You see?" she said. "You don't need anybody, do you?"

And went through the door, turning, pausing a moment to look at him, while out of the chilly darkness the mechanical bird sang its bright and manufactured note, and a part of the Investigator thought exultantly *I'm done with all of them now* and another part, like a man rooted in a dream, tried to call her name, to ask her to wait. But the words would not come. The bird scattered a shiny gravel of sound on the darkness and Lulubel said in a neutral voice: "Back to Amalgamated Joy or off to the Unoccupied Country. See you around, daddio," and closed the door after her.

———o———

Now that he was done with all of them the exultation went out of him and he felt apathetic. He went heavily over to the liquor cabinet and poured himself a large drink. Then, almost reluctantly, he went to the communicator and dialed the office. A sleepy clerk, the only man in the room, showed on the screen.

"Gannell," the Investigator said crisply. "Tell him to come out here. Tell him to bring Jones. Tell him if he's not here in two hours I'll have him arrested for conspiracy."

Sleep went out of the face of the frightened clerk. "Yes sir," he said. "Is there anything else?"

"That ought to bring him," Cary said dryly.

He sat back and finished his drink. He felt relaxed now that the money was down, almost sleepy. He sat there a while, dozing and drinking but there was still something he must do before Gannell came. What was it? Yes, now he remembered it, and he pulled himself up from the chair and put down his glass and went to his study.

There was something in his file that he must ask Gannell about. He pulled at his desk drawer—what was it he had to remember? Something back in his head buzzed a warning like an angry rattler. The drawer came open—

A long gaud of light slashed at his eyes and he thought in pure wonder *I'm shot I'm shot* even before pain came like an ax against his head. Then he dropped into the darkness.

————o————

He was aware of a strong light in his eyes and he wanted to get up but he couldn't. Did something move back there in the darkness, outside the circle of light? Did he hear a chair scrape?

"Who's there?" the Investigator asked of the darkness.

There was no answer.

"I know someone's there," the Investigator said. "I can tell about things like that."

Again nothing.

The Investigator laughed. "I know you," he said. "I have seen your iron outriders. I have been chained to your wheel of fire. I have been torn by your great beaked bird. You really came, didn't you? You are the Accuser who is god of this world."

Again there was silence. Then someone spoke: (Why could he not remember the voice? Cary wondered) "You know there are no gods of this world."

"Jones, then. The Grand Inquisitor."

"You know well enough who I am," the voice said. "What do you want?"

"I want nothing," the voice said indifferently. "I came here to ask what it is *you* want."

Now it seemed hard for the Investigator to think, to say, what he wanted. He knew what it was—something just there outside the circle of his thought, outside the light. . . .

"Order," he said. "I wanted everything to work out right. I wanted to *make* everything work out right. Justice, Good Engineering, proper procedures——" The words marched glibly off his tongue but somehow they were not quite what he wanted to say and he stopped.

"That's not enough to ask for," the indifferent voice

said. "Now, I'll give you nothing. Why not ask for perfection, since that is what you want? But whose perfection, eh? Or why not ask for Love? But, of course, Clarabel and your wife both offered that and you didn't want it, did you? Nor the friendship or solidarity or comradeship of Levin? Nor the wisdom of the past, present or future. So now I'll give you nothing."

"It's not fair," the Investigator said, aware that he was whimpering but not able to stop and not caring. "It's not fair. You're all against me. You tried to kill me. You _____"

"Nonsense," the voice said. "You're too good an Investigator not to know what happened. Who could have booby-trapped the time-file and the Psychomat? And you certainly recognized the voice that threatened you at the Club, didn't you?"

"No!" Cary shouted in terror. "No! It's not true! What about the order to close my brother's file?"

"Yes," the voice said. "It is true. Your brother is dead. It was simply a mistake that started up an investigation of him. Gannell was not working against you, nor Jones. You know who was responsible for everything."

"No!" Cary shouted again. "I'm not guilty!"

"Nonsense," the voice said again with the same indifference. "You're the only one who could have set traps for yourself. There's no plot against you except the one you imagined and made for yourself."

"No!" Cary said. He was sobbing without control now. "I didn't mean to. It isn't my fault. Nobody ever loved me!"

"You never let anyone love you."

"No one——"

124

"You can't be excused that way," the voice said patiently. "Many are unloved or think they are, but they do not do what you did. And anyway, didn't you profit from the kind of society you helped create? Isn't it true that you acted out of ambition, and the desire for power, and that you treated men as if they were machines, without love?"

"I took nothing," Cary said. "Others enriched themselves. I was indifferent——"

"You were indifferent to men. Indifference without solidarity is an evil thing. Didn't the Preacher tell you that, and the Sibyl?"

"It can't be true," Cary said. "Why would I do that to myself, trap myself that way?"

"That should be easiest of all for you to understand," the voice told him. "Isn't the perfect hunter always interested in a more difficult kind of game to stalk? And who would be harder for you to catch than yourself?"

"But I wouldn't——"

"It's perfectly logical to an Investigator's way of thinking. If everyone is guilty, either now or later, and if everyone is to be suspected, you will have to suspect yourself in the end. You thought with perfect logic—for an Investigator. Isn't it proper that your ultimate victim should be yourself?"

"But I didn't catch myself," Cary said. "You are the Accuser, the Grand Inquisitor. Otherwise——"

"Otherwise you have trapped yourself. That is true. You were your own victim, as I have told you."

"Then," Cary said. "Then—in that case——" An awful terror took hold of him. He tried again to rise, but he could not. "In that case—*you are me!*"

125

"Of course," the voice said out of the darkness. "Now you have everything perfectly in order."

———o———

The Investigator came slowly back to consciousness. By degrees the room swam into fixity and shape, first the overhead light, then the dark bulge of the desk which loomed over him like a cliff. He put his hand to his head and it came away thick and sticky with blood, but his head itself was quite numb.

He could not think what could have happened to him. Then he remembered: the drawer, the trap-gun he had set for Gannell or Jones a few hours earlier. How could he have forgotten it? he wondered; he had trapped himself——

Trapped himself! The thought seemed to explode inside his head. He sat up, looking. There was no one there. Now, infinitely more painful than the wound, the memory of the Accuser came back to his mind; and then something more awful still: there had been no Accuser. No one had been talking to him. It had been a dream—a nightmare. But it was worse than any nightmare, because all of it was true.

Slowly he got to his feet and dragged himself into the living room and sat down. There was nothing to do now but wait. There had been no plot—only his own conspiracy against himself—the ultimate sedition. It would be enough for Gannell or for Jones, if there was a Jones. There was nothing to do now but wait.

Now the winter was past, and the long cold rains, and the Workless Stiffs, increased in numbers, a bit more defiant, were again enjoying the freedom of the park. In the early dusk the lights of their little fires dotted the square. Above them the tin trees wore their new tin spring green leaves with an air of civic pride; the robot squirrels gathered their plastic acorns with a jolly mechanical briskness, whisking their nylon tails. Somewhere in the growing dusk a bird sang one clear note and then was silent as if his current had been cut off abruptly. In a corner of the park, an old man mounted a bench and began to talk:

"Brothers, the day is come, the time of the Destroyer, the time of that dark and hunted man who lives in all of us, the time when everything shall be made level, all roads straight, and man shall say again the great Aleph of solidarity——"

The angry voice punched at the indifferent air and now a ring of men began to gather around the speaker. Farther off, men lay under the bushes and talked quietly, heating their coffee in tin cans. Somewhere a harmonica began, a melancholy blues: "O her love will get it, till its tall as a Georgia pine"; the sound floated on the blue air.

A man came into the park, walking with some uncertainty, wearing the bemused air of a saint or an idiot or a man who had been juiced. It was the Investigator. One of the Workless Stiffs recognized him and spat, but the Investigator did not notice. He went tiredly to a bench and sat down, pulling his shabby coat around himself. The song drifted to him on the twilight air and lighted up, just for a moment, the memory of a girl, blonde, beautiful, somehow—misplaced. Most of his memories seemed misplaced nowadays. He remembered the smell of coffee and it made him hungry. Somewhere a bird sang down its round emphatic note. It seemed to the Investigator that, once, somewhere, he had heard a bird sing just like that.

THE END